I want an **ALIEN** for *Christmas*

by

Nick Santora

TELEMACHUS PRESS

This book is a work of fiction. Names, characters, places and incidents are either the product of the author's imagination or are used fictitiously. Any resemblance to actual persons, living or dead, or to actual events or locales is entirely coincidental.

The publisher does not have any control over and does not assume any responsibility for author or third-party websites or their content.

Cover art and design by Noelle Raffaele

Published by Telemachus Press, LLC
http://www.telemachuspress.com

ISBN: 978-1-941536-26-1 (eBook)
ISBN: 978-1-941536-27-8 (Paperback)

Version 2014.06.28

Printed in the United States of America

10 9 8 7 6 5 4 3 2 1

For my little aliens

I want an **ALIEN** for *Christmas*

CHAPTER 1
AN EXPLOSION IN THE WOODS

THE *CRASH* THAT twelve-year-old Theo Bartlett and his sisters heard on the night of December 17th seemed louder than the last ten seconds of a 4th of July show when the fireworks guy sets off all the cool rockets he has left all at once. Or maybe it just seemed that loud because the *BANG* came out of nowhere on such a quiet night.

It was about a second after Olivia (Theo's ten-year-old sister and constant pain in the neck) and Sophie (his five year old sister and constant pain in the butt) put the finishing touches on *Mr. Whitey* that the *BAM* shook the ground so hard that the snowman tipped over—his head rolling one way, his body rolling the other.

"Mr. Whitey's dead!" Sophie screamed. Then she laughed wildly and leapt onto Mr. Whitey's head, backside first, crushing the snowman's face.

"Don't slam the door, kids. You just rattled the whole house!" they heard their father call from inside. "And it's getting late—time for baths and bed!"

"But Dad, we didn't slam the door."

"Don't argue with me, Theo. One of these days you're going to knock that thing right off its hinges."

Theo shook his head in frustration. He was always getting blamed for things he didn't do ... or at least it felt that way.

"Maybe it was an earthquake," Olivia piped in. She was always chiming in with little facts and figures and sciencey stuff that Theo couldn't have cared less about.

"Yeah, maybe it was an earthcake," Sophie mimicked. She copied Olivia a lot—and since Theo thought Olivia was one of the most annoying people in the world, that just made Sophie the *second* most annoying person in the world.

"There aren't earthquakes in New Hampshire, Einstein," Theo mocked as he trudged through the snow toward their father's shed.

"Actually," Olivia countered as she followed her brother, "there are fault lines all over the eastern seaboard, and seismic activity, though rare ..."

"—Whatever, Professor," Theo interrupted as he opened the shed and pulled down a flashlight from a hook on the back of the door.

"Where are you going?" Olivia asked.

"Crazy," Theo wisecracked. "Wanna come?" He headed toward the woods.

"We're not allowed in the woods at night. And Dad said we need to get in."

"Then just Sophie and I will go," Theo said smiling at his baby sister. He didn't really care if she came with him or not. He just knew that Olivia *didn't* want Sophie to go. "I'll need an *Executive Assistant Explorer.*"

Sophie's eyes glistened—she liked the sound of that! She followed her big brother into the trees.

"Wait!" Olivia worried. "You can't go with him, you're too little."

"I'm not little," Sophie protested. "I'm the *Electric Assistant Exploder,*" she said proudly. Then she bounded after Theo. Olivia watched them disappear into the tree line. Theo was always doing things like this—making dumb decisions and then mocking her for not doing the same. It made her so mad. She didn't *hate* him—he was her brother after all—but sometimes she just didn't *like* him.

"Guys?" she called out softly, but Theo and Sophie were out of earshot. She looked around, realizing she was alone in the very dark corner of the backyard. The wind pushed the shed door back and forth just a bit—*creeeeak.* Olivia swallowed hard and then raced after her brother and sister. "Wait up!"

After running for just about fifteen seconds she spotted the beam from Theo's flashlight not too far ahead and caught up easily.

"The sound came from deeper in the woods, past the creek," Theo said with authority, though he wasn't really sure.

So they kept walking, further into the woods, farther from home. The snow was deep and crunched heavy beneath their feet though you couldn't really hear it because with every step Sophie would sing:

Crunch.

Scrunch.

Bunch.

Lunch.

Or any other word that rhymed.

They passed the Old Face Tree—a massive dying oak whose grooves and knots made the trunk look like the face of a tired old man. *Old Face* kind of creeped out Theo, even in the daytime, so he made sure not to shine his flashlight on it.

They climbed up and over Miller's Hill—a mountain of earth that grew nothing but weeds but provided a great launching off point for bike riders brave enough to risk flying head-on into the patch of pricker bushes that grew at the base. Theo had seen many a daredevil walk away from a Miller Hill jump looking more porcupine than human.

And finally, they crossed over Crooked Creek, so named because it snaked all through the town of Millbrook Falls—around trees, under bridges and through farms until it eventually reached the Falls themselves, where it emptied into the bed of the Granite River.

The three Bartlett kids eventually reached an area that was more forest than woods—the trees were dense and thick with evergreen needles and despite the flashlight, they couldn't find anything that could've caused the noise they had heard.

"Can we go home now, please?" Olivia asked. "There's nothing here."

"There's got to be something," Theo countered, his eyes squinting, searching the dark for a clue. "You don't get a loud noise unless something goes with it."

"What about a toot?" Sophie said. "When I eat prunes, I make loud toots and nothing goes with it. It's just a noise."

"Really?" Theo answered frustrated. "You think what we heard was just the woods *farting?*"

Sophie giggled. "You said *fart*."

"Fine, let's go home." Theo turned to leave. Olivia followed; glad to be heading back to the house. But Sophie didn't move.

"Let's not go yet," she said, looking at something in the distance, wide-eyed with excitement. "Let's open *that* first."

"Open what?" Olivia asked.

"*That*," Sophie pointed.

Theo aimed the flashlight beam in the direction of Sophie's finger. It landed about 50 feet away … resting on a perfectly wrapped Christmas present sticking halfway out of the snow.

"What the …?" Theo said. But he didn't finish his thought because Sophie was already hurrying through the snow to the pretty box, wrapped in silver paper with a red bow.

"*Don't touch it*," Olivia warned.

"Why not?" Sophie asked.

"Because it doesn't belong to us."

The three kids just looked at the present for a moment, none of them saying anything. The moonlight reflected off the shiny paper, pulled tightly around the box. It was the most impeccably wrapped gift any of them had ever seen.

"There's another one!" Sophie exclaimed, pointing to a red and green box sticking out of a snowdrift a few feet away.

"Over there!" yelled Olivia, spotting a long, rectangular box leaning against a tree.

"Over here!" shouted Theo, racing to a circular gift wrapped in red tissue paper with green yarn bows on either side.

And so it went. The three of them plucked Christmas presents from the snow and snagged them from low hanging branches. By the time they reached a remote clearing they all had their arms full of boxes, piled so high they had to peek around them to see where they were walking.

And that's when they saw the sleigh.

CHAPTER 2

THE OUTER SPACE SNOT ROCKET

"SANTA!" SOPHIE SCREAMED before dropping all of her gift-wrapped treasures and running to the massive sleigh (which was dark red with brilliant gold trim). The front of the sleigh was smashed into a tree trunk. In the back was a huge, green, velvet sack with white piping—it had presents in it and even more presents were strewn about on the ground. Sophie climbed up onto the sleigh and looked inside. For a kid that was a few months shy of turning six, she wasn't scared of anything.

"He's not here," she said, disappointed.

"How'd this thing get all the way out here in the middle of nowhere?" Theo asked. Olivia slowly stepped closer, stopping when she spotted something way off in the distance, behind the sleigh.

"Are those … I think those are … over there … are those _reindeer_ eating berries from those bushes?!" she asked amazed.

"Reindeer!" Sophie smiled. "Rudolph!"

Theo squinted his eyes. He could see the forms of some kind of animals in the distance, but it was dark and they were a few hundred feet away.

"They're pretty big alright, but they're not reindeer," he said.

"How do you know?"

"Because, Liv, there aren't any reindeer in Millbrook Falls. Regular deer? Loads of 'em. But reindeer? I don't think so."

"But the sled. The presents. What looks like reindeer. Don't you think … just maybe … that this sleigh could be … _his?_" Olivia asked.

Theo looked at his sister … and then _burst out laughing!_

"Whose? _Santa's?_ Yeah, this is Santa's sleigh and over by the creek I think I saw the Easter Bunny's _motorcycle_—"

"—It's not funny—"

"—and right over there is the Tooth Fairy's submarine!"

"Then how do you explain all this?" Olivia asked.

"Yeah, how do you 'splain all this?" Sophie echoed.

"It's a display from a shopping center or something," Theo argued. "I bet some teenagers hitched it up to their snowmobiles and took it for a joyride."

Olivia pointed to two deep grooves in the snow that stretched from the sleigh's runners all the way to the middle of the clearing ... *and then stopped.*

"Then what about the sleigh tracks?" she asked. "They start right over there, like this sleigh just *crash landed* and skidded to a stop."

"You know, for a know-it-all, straight-A student, you're pretty dumb, sis," Theo countered. "It's <u>*snowing*</u>. The tracks were filled in with snow and this part here is taking longer to fill up because they're under the trees. Man, I can understand Sophie believing in Santa, but you're 10 years old. You should know better. This sleigh was swiped by some dopes who crashed it into that tree. <u>That</u> was the noise we heard. That's it. Case solved."

"But you don't think it's strange ...'"

"No!" Theo had had enough—he was cold and tired of talking about an imaginary man in a red suit. "I'm telling you for the last time, there's nothing strange about this sleigh."

... And that's when they heard the sound coming from the large velvet bag.

Gug-guggle. Mug-a-gug.

It was a low, rumbling kind of noise—the presents in the bag began to shift and move around a bit—there was someone, or *something*, in the sack. The kids all froze—it was silent for a moment. Then they heard it again—

Guggle-muggle. Gug-guggle-muggle.

"That doesn't sound like Santa," Sophie said quietly.

"*I told you there was something going on with this sleigh,*" Olivia whispered to Theo. Theo was just as scared as any of them—but he couldn't let his sisters know it—and, more importantly, he couldn't let Olivia think she was right. So he slowly approached the back of the sleigh. "It's probably just a squirrel stuck in there. I'll let him out and we can go home."

He stepped carefully to make as little "crunching" sound as possible in the snow. Just as he reached the bag and peered over the side of the sleigh, the movement inside the bag stopped. Theo took a deep breath.

"See it was nothing …"

"*Guuuuuuuuug!*"

Something BURST out of the bag, sending presents flying everywhere. It was small and green with big eyes and two antennae growing from the top of either side of his head. Each antennae, dropped and hung over, like floppy bunny ears, except the ends were shaped like the opening of a small trumpet. "*Guuuuuuuuuug!*" it shouted again.

"*Aaaaaaaagh!*" Theo screamed.

"*Guuuuuuuug!*" the creature screamed back, but this time *thick green gunk* shot out of its trumpet-horn-antennae and splattered all over Theo's face.

"*Aaaaaaaagh!*" Olivia and Sophie cried.

"*Eeeeeewwww! He gorked all over me!*" Theo howled in a panic.

"*Guuuuuuuug!*" the creature wailed once more before awkwardly falling out of the sleigh and into the snow, trying to waddle away as fast as it could. But it only took a few steps before tripping on one of the presents and letting out a cry of "*Guggle!*" before his thick-toed feet flew out from under him and he fell face-first into the snow. He scurried onto his back and looked at the three kids with wide, frightened eyes.

As Theo wiped the gunk from his face, his sisters got a good look at the creature cowering a few feet away from them.

"He's scared," Olivia said softly.

"Don't be afraid," Sophie hushed as she approached the strange little fellow.

"Sophie, don't …" Theo said, but his sister had already plopped herself next to the small, green guy. She reached out and gently touched his hand. It felt rubbery, kind of like the stingrays in the petting pond at Nashua Aquarium. He didn't pull away.

"We're nice," Sophie continued. "We won't hurt you." With Sophie next to him, it was clear how actually <u>un</u>-scary the creature was. He wasn't much bigger than she was, maybe about 4 feet high. He had hands and feet that were a little too big for his body and wide, expressive eyes—the eyes of, well, a *kid*.

Sophie instantly liked him, and he liked her too. He could tell that even though two of the pale creatures staring at him were bigger than he was, they were not a danger.

"You have a boo-boo?" Sophie asked, pointing to a cut on his forehead, which oozed a blue sludge. "I can fix that for you. I have a doctor's kit at home."

"*Home?* Are you crazy?" Theo asked. "We can't take this thing *home*."

"He's not a <u>thing</u>," Sophie defended. "He's ..." Sophie wasn't sure how to finish that sentence, so she turned to her new friend. "I'm *SOPHIE*," she said, pronouncing her name slowly and loudly. "Who are *you?*"

The green visitor just looked at her. He didn't understand a word she was saying. "Gug?" he asked confused.

"His name's Gug," Olivia said definitively, as she knelt next to him. "And he does have a bad bruise. We should help."

"You're out of your mind!" Theo yelled. "He could be radioactive for all we know! We don't even know <u>what</u> he is!"

"Yes we do," Olivia said looking at Gug with wonder. She turned to her brother and stared him in the eyes. "He's an alien—from outer space. Unless you want to try to convince me he's just a regular, old deer too." Olivia was dead serious and Theo couldn't argue with her because right there in front of him was the proof—a little *something* with sagging horn-ears who bled blue blood and sprayed green gunk. There was no denying it. This wasn't a dream. This wasn't his imagination. This was real! Theo was speechless.

"How'd you get here?" Sophie asked Gug, once again talking too slowly and loudly, as if "slow and loud" was the key to intergalactic language barriers.

Olivia tried to help. She pointed to the sleigh. "Is this yours?" she asked.

Even though he didn't comprehend the words Olivia was saying, Gug could tell she wanted to know if that big contraption belonged to him.

"Gug gug goo, gug-a-goo."

All he got was blank stares. No point in trying to talk to them, Gug thought. Then he had an idea. He jumped up (startling Theo who quickly took a step back) and leapt onto the sleigh and into the velvet bag. He scrounged around for a few moments and then reappeared with a large doll in a beautiful red petticoat.

"*A Candy Calloway doll,*" Olivia said wistfully to herself. She'd always wanted a Candy Calloway of her own.

Gug put on the red petticoat and then grabbed a section of black, rubber racetrack from a Speedster 5000 Triple Loop Stunt Man Set and tied it tightly around his waist to look like a belt. He hopped back to the ground and grabbed handfuls of snow and caked them onto his face, starting just under his wide nose, across his cheeks and up to the base of his horn-ears, which grew upward, starting a few inches above where human ears would've been if he were indeed human. When he was done, he had a long, thick snow-beard.

With the beard, the red coat and the black belt, Gug looked just like …

"Santa!" Sophie shouted.

Olivia shot Theo an "I told you so" look.

Gug hopped into the front seat of the sleigh and pretended to steer. "*Gug, gug, gug!*" he said in a deep, jovial voice—it sounded very much like "*Ho, ho, ho!*"

Then he pulled a Wham-O Frisbee out of the bag, knocked the snow beard off his face and hopped onto the Frisbee. He pretended to hold an invisible steering wheel.

"You were driving your space ship?" Olivia put together.

Gug jumped up and put on another snow beard. "Gug, gug, gug," he ho-ho-ho'd again as he pantomimed guiding the sled. But this time he picked up his Frisbee and *smashed it* into the sleigh. By the way Gug did this, it was clear he felt the driver of the sleigh was the responsible party for the accident.

"BA-GUUUUG!" he cried out, doing the best he could to mimic the sound of a collision.

"I think I understand," Olivia said. "Gug, you were on some kind of space vehicle (she held up the Frisbee) and you crashed into this sleigh (she pointed to the sleigh) and you wound up in here (she pointed to the velvet bag) … But where's the man in the red suit?"

Gug just looked at her—he couldn't understand.

"Where's this man?" Olivia tried again as she deepened her voice for a hearty *"Ho, ho, ho!"* "Where's the man who says *that?*"

Gug understood what she was asking. He picked up the Frisbee and pointed to it, then pointed up high in the sky.

"Oh no," Olivia deduced. "The crash made Santa tumble into the space craft and Gug fall into the sleigh. He crashed *here* and Santa is still somewhere *up there.*"

"Santa's at the Millbrook Falls Mall taking pictures with kids dumb enough to believe in him for five bucks a pop," Theo said sarcastically.

"So you can believe in aliens, but not Santa?" Olivia countered.

"Yeah," Theo answered. "Because this green guy's right here, in front of my eyes. I can see him. He's not some guy parents created to bribe their kids with presents so they'll be good one month out of the year."

"*Ooooooh*, you're gonna get coal, Theo," Sophie warned.

Theo continued, "This Gug guy's from somewhere other than here, and he had the bad luck of landing in a hijacked sled that was abandoned in the woods."

"Then who is Gug pretending to be when he puts on the red jacket and beard?"

"I don't know," Theo responded. "Maybe he just likes to dress up." But Theo was starting to doubt himself—the sleigh; the presents; Gug's impersonation of someone who looked a heck of a lot like Santa; and maybe those *were* reindeer wandering off into the woods. *No!* It couldn't be. Theo only believed in things he could see and hear and touch—things that are real, things that are right in front of his eyes blowing snot rockets all over his face. That's what's real!

As crazy as it was to believe, there was an alien standing with them in the woods. *That* he couldn't deny. So he wouldn't. But he wasn't about to admit that *Santa Claus* was real. He was twelve years old for Pete's sake! He had stopped believing in Santa Claus a long time ago! But … it all was a pretty strange coincidence. Theo would admit at least that.

He looked at the alien for a moment—poor Gug had been through a lot—he was hurt and scared and tired. Theo softened a bit. "I guess we can't just leave him out here—he'll freeze to death."

Sophie and Olivia smiled.

"But we can't let Mom and Dad know," Theo stressed. "They'd ground us until *next* Christmas if they found out we were in the woods at night again. We'll fix him up, feed him, and then tomorrow dump him back out here."

"No," Olivia said, stepping in front of Gug defensively. Sophie did the same. "Don't you see what's going on? Gug needs to get back home. And Santa needs to get back to his sleigh!"

Olivia leaned in toward her brother and looked him right in the eye; she had never been more serious about anything in her life.

"Listen closely, Theo," she said. "We have one week to track down Gug's ship, find Santa Claus and *save Christmas*!"

CHAPTER 3
THE DECAPITATED SNOWMAN

THEO DIDN'T ARGUE with Olivia. He knew what she was like when she put her mind to something. She was like their dad that way. Mr. Bartlett was a professional magician, and not a very good one. He could do the basic tricks—pull rubber chickens from hats, the disappearing ball, "_this_ is your card." But when it came to any sophisticated illusion, he could never get it right. But he <u>never</u> gave up. _Never._ He'd spend months working on something, and if he couldn't master it, then he'd work on it for a year. In fact, New Year's would mark the five-year anniversary of their dad trying to perform the stunt called _"The Big Goodbye"_—with no success. But he never quit. And Olivia didn't either—she'd inherited Mr. Bartlett's determination. So that's how Theo found himself walking down Franklin Avenue at nine o'clock at night with Gug sandwiched in between all three of them to hide him from any cars that might pass by.

Theo had decided they should cut through the woods to the street and then walk around the block back to their house. That way, if the cops found the stolen sleigh from the mall they wouldn't track a fresh path in the snow back to where they lived. It was a cold night in the middle of winter so there was no one on the road. It seemed like a perfect plan ... until they spotted Winston Polenski heading right for them from the other end of the block.

Winston was the biggest bully at Eisenhower Memorial School. He was so mean that the _other_ bullies called him "Mr. Polenski" and even some of the teachers seemed intimidated by him. Mr. Wickman, the science teacher, gave Winston a 98 on a Solar System Project that was nothing but Styrofoam balls held together with bent coat hangers. It deserved a 70 at best. But Winston was five inches taller than the next biggest kid in the class and a full inch taller than Mr. Wickman himself, so there you go—a 98 for mediocre work. Theo's vinegar and baking soda-powered volcano only got an 85. That still bothered him.

Even the local football league had to change the rules. Normally, if you were 12 years old or less, you played in the Pony Conference. Problem was, no one in the Pony Conference could tackle Winston. Every match eventually became a game of chase—Winston would get the ball and 11 kids from the other team would chase him all the way down the field to the end zone. Sometimes, Winston would plod along with two or three kids clinging to his waist and legs, but he'd never go down. So the league put Winston in the Mustang Conference with 13, 14 and 15 year old teenagers. Everyone knew this would even things out—there was no way Winston would be able to run over boys that were years older than him.

In his first game in the Mustang Conference, Winston scored 4 touchdowns.

"Oh no, it's Winston," Theo whispered.

"We're in between street lamps so he doesn't see us yet!" Olivia whispered back.

Theo spun his head back and forth—no bushes, no big trees, no parked cars. "There's no place to hide!" he cried.

"The snowman!" Sophie said, pointing to a snowman in a second-hand, blue, wool jacket, a red hat with earflaps on top and a thick scarf with mittens.

Thinking the snowman was real, Gug waved at it. "Guggity goo," was his *hello*.

"It's not big enough for all of us to hide behind," Theo responded.

"No," Sophie answered, frustrated. "The *snowman*."

It was then that Theo understood what his sister was trying to tell him.

Winston Polenski saw the kids walking his way when he got about halfway down the block. He recognized Theo as the dorky kid he was always picking on, and whose hockey team hadn't won a game in over a year. And he knew Olivia from school—she was a brainiac who was always studying and getting awards at assembly time. And the little kid, he didn't know her name, but he saw her with Theo and Olivia a lot—she was the weirdo who liked to spin around on playground equipment until she was dizzy and then try to chase squirrels.

But Winston didn't recognize the fourth kid that was with them. He was wearing a wool jacket that was so big on him that it almost dragged on the ground and a hat pulled way down to just above his eyes and a scarf wrapped so high around his neck that you couldn't see the kid's face.

"Hey *Fart*lett, it's a little late for you, ain't it? Don't you know it's dangerous to be out at night by yourself?" Winston said threateningly.

"Our name's not *Fart*lett, it's Bartlett," Olivia corrected indignantly.

"Yeah," Sophie protested. "Farts come from your butt. *We* come from our *parents*."

Winston looked quizzically at Sophie and then turned back to Theo. "Who's the new dorkling, Fartlett?"

"Um, that's our friend. He's um …, he's uhh …"

"Didn't ask for his life story, Turdzilla." Winston directed his attention to Gug. "What's your problem, you don't talk?"

"Gugga gugga goo-goo," Gug said, his voice muffled from the scarf.

"You some kind of a funny guy?" Winston said. "How's this for funny?" he asked as he turned and punched the head right off the snowman.

Thinking the snowman was real and had just been *murdered*, Gug let out a loud cry and his antennae instantly shot thick green goop out from under his hat—*right into Winston's face*. Gug didn't mean to do it, but when he got scared or excited, the goop always started flying!

"*Uuuugh!*" Winston cried.

As Winston tried to wipe the thick gunk from his eyes, Theo knew this was their chance to get away. He grabbed Sophie by the hand and ran across the street. Olivia followed with Gug. Behind them you could hear Winston scream, "You're dead, Bartlett! No one blows snot in Winston Polenski's face!"

Gug and the kids were halfway across the street when a beat up Oldsmobile *screeched* to a stop, just inches away from them.

"Hey you kids! What are you, crazy?! You coulda got killed!"

Theo knew the man was right—his parents had told him a million times to look both ways before crossing the street but he was so desperate to get Gug away from Winston that he wasn't even thinking straight.

"Sorry!" Theo shouted over his shoulder without stopping as he ran home with Olivia, Sophie and an alien dressed in snowman's clothes.

CHAPTER 4
GRUMPY OLD SAINT NICK

ARTIE SNEED WAS still grumbling to himself four blocks after almost hitting those kids with his car. *Kids!* He hated them! They were the worst people on earth! They thought the whole world revolved around them! Especially during Christmas time—*Bring me this Santa; Get me that Santa; I want, I want, I want!!* The only thing Artie hated more than kids was Christmas!

If he were in charge of things, the first thing he'd do would be to get rid of that holiday. He'd pass a law against giving presents, putting up trees, hanging lights, singing carols, baking holiday fruitcake and doing anything else that had to do with Christmas.

If he saw someone so much as carry a stocking within five feet of a fireplace, he'd have that person arrested. Eating a candy cane would get you twenty years in prison! Owning tinsel would carry a life sentence!

Christmas would be illegal!

Artie grinned fiendishly at the thought, but after a moment he had to stop. He grinned and smiled so seldom that when he actually did, it hurt his face. Besides, there was no point in thinking about a world without Christmas—that dream would never come true.

As he pulled his clunker of a car into the Millbrook Falls Mall parking lot, Artie sighed. He knew that he was stuck with Christmas—there was nothing he could do about it.

"You are **late**—once again!" a voice called out as Artie parked his car. Artie looked out of his car window to find a very angry, very thin and very bald man hurrying toward him. It was his boss, Mr. Lipson, and he was waving a piece of paper over his head.

"Your employment agreement clearly states that your shift begins at 9:00 pm sharp. Do you know what time it is?"

Artie wiped spittle from his face as Mr. Lipson had the habit of spitting a little when he talked.

"Christmas time?" Artie wisecracked as he climbed out of his car.

"Don't get smart with me," Mr. Lipson said looking Artie up and down with disgust. "You're unkempt, disheveled, unshaven ... now just hurry up and get inside. But one more mistake and you're fired. I swear you're the worst person I've ever had in this job. Thank goodness it's only seasonal!"

Lipson turned and began walking quickly back to the mall. Artie adjusted the buckle on his thick belt, pulled his jacket down over his belly and reached back into his car for his cap, which he plopped down onto his head.

He still couldn't believe that this was the only paying gig he could find. But he'd been fired from his last three places of employment for having a negative attitude and being overly surly to his fellow workers. *Overly surly to fellow workers?* Well if they thought that he was surly, then they were just a bunch of stupid idiots!

Now fully dressed and ready for work, Artie Sneed slowly and unenthusiastically followed after his boss through the parking lot toward the mall. He walked slowly because he knew after a few more feet he would step through large glass doors and into one of the most horrible jobs he could ever have asked for ... Department Store Santa Claus.

CHAPTER 5
THE ICELANDIC EXCHANGE
STUDENT

SOPHIE HAD HER face pressed up hard against the kitchen window. Theo, Olivia and Gug were hiding in the bushes a few feet away.

"What do you see?" Theo asked.

"My breath!" Sophie answered. "Look!" She pointed excitedly to where she had fogged up the windowpane by breathing onto it.

"No," Olivia corrected, exasperated. "What do you see _inside_ the house?"

"Oh," Sophie said. "I see Mommy making chocolate Christmas tree cookies—the ones with M&M's on top for the star. Mmmmmmmmmm ..."

"_Focus_," Theo whispered. "Is Dad in there?"

"Nope."

"I don't know how we're going to just sneak Gug past her," Theo worried.

Sophie turned back toward the window, salivating at the sight of all those cookies just an arm's reach away on the other side of the glass ... _so close, yet so far._ She leaned in closer, as if she could somehow taste the fresh-out-of-the-oven-treats until ... _thump_—she knocked her forehead into the pane.

One of the Bartlett's six dogs heard this and picked up his head. _Woof!_ Then the other five hounds lifted their heads—_WOOF!!!_ Then they all ran to the window to find the three kids and Gug outside by the bushes.

WOOFWOOFWOOFWOOFWOOFWOOFWOOF!! The dogs went wild!

Gug shrieked and blew gunk all over the glass pane! Theo grabbed him by the arm and yanked him around to the other side of the house. Olivia and Sophie were right behind them!

"That was close!" Olivia panted.

They could hear their mother scolding the dogs. "Silly doggies, you can't get those gophers. They're *outside*, and you're *inside*. And lucky for you, isn't it, you little *poochie-woochies* 'cause you get *treaty-weeties* in here where it's all *warmsy-pormsy*."

As the kids listened to Mrs. Bartlett give the dogs some Milk-Bones, Theo was struck with an idea.

"That's it! The dogs!" he said.

"Mom and Dad will not believe Gug is a dog!" Olivia said incredulously.

"No. Just a few years ago, we only had one dog—now we have *six*; by the time Sophie graduates high school our house will be a kennel."

"So, Mom likes to take in strays …"

"Exactly," Theo said, eyes gleaming with the energy of a great idea. "So let's give her a stray she couldn't possibly say no to."

As the kids made their way to the front of the house, Theo explained his plan. Olivia hated to admit it, but it was a pretty good one. It was still a long shot, but it was the only chance they had.

They all quietly entered the house. Gug looked around in wonder at the home—it was so different from the three story, levitating, hydrogen pod he and his family lived in back on his home planet. He spotted the large, lit-up Christmas tree in the corner.

"Gaaaaaaa," he cooed in wonderment. He quickly waddled over to it.

"Stay with him," Theo whispered to Sophie. Sophie chased after her new alien friend, giggling, as Theo reached outside, rang the doorbell and then closed the door.

"Coming," they heard their mother call from the kitchen.

Theo hurried over to the tree where Gug's face was now glowing— *from the inside*—because he was happily stuffing a long strand of Christmas lights into his mouth!

"Why'd you let him do that?" Theo scolded Sophie as he grabbed a hold of the lights.

"'Cause it's funny," Sophie giggled.

Theo pulled on the lights, but Gug's head just yanked forward—the whole strand stayed in his mouth lit up.

Sophie pressed a button and the *lights started to blink*. Gug's cheeks lit up red, orange, yellow, blue, green, and pink.

"He looks like a traffic light!" Sophie squealed.

"You're not helping," Theo yelled. "If mom sees this, we're as good as dead. Olivia, grab his waist."

Olivia grabbed Gug from behind to hold him steady and Theo yanked on the light strand as hard as he could. He flew backwards with the strand in his hands as the bulbs popped out of Gug's mouth one by one— *POPPOPPOPPOPPOPPOPPOPPOP!*

Theo landed on his butt with a thud just as his mother reached the front door.

"Oh, hello. What's going on here?" she asked.

Olivia jumped in front of Gug and quickly fixed the scarf around his face and pulled his hat down even tighter. He looked just like any other kid dressed for winter.

"Oh, uh, we just got kind of tangled up in the Christmas lights," Theo said.

"I think it's a little late to be having friends over," Mrs. Bartlett said, smiling at Gug. "Is that who rang the doorbell?"

"Yeah, this is my friend Gug, uh, *Gazinski*," Theo said. "Gug Gazinski. He's an exchange student from Iceland."

"Iceland? How interesting! How exotic!" Mrs. Bartlett said. She had always wanted to travel the world but had never been able to do so. She thought people from Canada were "exotic".

"Yeah, but here's the problem, Mom," Theo said. "He was staying with Mrs. Bottleman, and you know how rich they are and how they're always going away for Christmas vacation."

"Yes. I heard last year they went to *Chile*. Just like we put on our hot dogs!"

"Yeah, well, this year they're off to Tahiti or something and they said they could only bring family and so they left Gug here all by himself. He has no place to spend Christmas."

Now, Mrs. Bartlett was a kind woman. A sweet woman. The kind of woman that other kids wished was their mother after they'd spent an afternoon playing at the Bartlett home. She had a saying; *"A smile, a hug and hot cocoa in a mug—that'll fix almost anything that's troubling you."*

But when she heard that a young boy her son's age was left behind, all alone, in a strange country, *at Christmas* ... well, let's just say Mrs. Bottleman was lucky she was in Tahiti (though she really wasn't) or Mrs. Bartlett would've tracked her down and given her a piece of her mind.

"They left him?!" she shrieked.

"Just left him," Theo fibbed.

"But there's still a few days before school ends for the holiday break! Who will care for him?! Who will he spend Christmas with?!"

"Well," Olivia chimed in, "they left a bunch of cans of tuna fish for him, and for company they said he could watch as much TV as he wanted."

Theo could barely stifle a laugh when he saw his mother's reaction.

"What?!" she shouted. "That's horrible! Just terrible! It's unacceptable is what it is! Utterly unacceptable!"

All of Mrs. Bartlett's motherly instincts kicked into high gear and she turned to Gug and put her hand on his shoulder. Olivia's eyes grew wide in her head. She wondered if her mom could feel Gug's alien body through the thick winter coat.

"Oh, Gug, sweetheart, would you like to stay with us during Christmas? There's always room at our table for one more. And we'd love to have you."

Gug could tell right away that Mrs. Bartlett was kind. There was something about her that seemed soothing and familiar. Then Gug realized what it was—she reminded him of his own mother.

"Gazoo," Gug said softly.

"That means *yes*," Theo said.

"You speak Icelandic?" Mrs. Bartlett answered.

"We learned some in school, in anticipation of Gug's arrival," said Theo.

"My, my," his mother said, impressed.

"Googaly Boogaly Boo," Sophie said. "That's Iceland talk for—*Wanna go upstairs?*"

Mrs. Bartlett smiled at her youngest child. "Oh, is it now?" she said with a wink. "Well go on up and I'll come up to tuck you guys in in an hour or so."

As Mrs. Bartlett moved back to the kitchen the children sprinted to the steps, amazed that their plan worked.

"That was my *momma*," Sophie explained to Gug. "Do you have a *momma?*"

But before Gug could answer, he bumped headfirst into … *Mr. Bartlett* who was descending the stairs, deep in thought and, as usual, not paying much attention to what he was doing.

"*Oooof,*" he said, holding his stomach where Gug's thick head had struck him.

"Oh, uh, hi Dad," Theo and Olivia said at almost the same time.

"Hi Daddy," Sophie added.

"Hey kids," Mr. Bartlett said. "Oh, hello? Who's your pal here?"

"Gug."

"Gug?" Mr. Bartlett responded to the strange name. "Okay. Well, Gug, you wanna see a trick?"

"He doesn't speak English," Olivia explained quickly, just wanting to get out of there.

"He's from Icelandia," Sophie added.

"No matter," Mr. Bartlett said dramatically. "Because *magic* is the universal language!" He stood and raised his hands high in the air. Olivia knew what was coming. *Oh no*, she thought, *not The Big Goodbye.*

"This, Gug, is called The Big Goodbye," he proclaimed proudly. "I've been working on it all day …"

"And the five years *before* today," Theo cracked quietly to Olivia.

"Ready?" Mr. Bartlett announced. "One. *Two.* **Three!** *ARAZMATAZ!!*" He swung his arms down quickly and stood there triumphantly.

Nothing happened.

Nothing at all.

Then, a few small streams of smoke slowly began to curl their way out of his sleeves and float toward the ceiling.

"Gagul?" Gug said to Sophie, confused.

"Don't ask me. I've never seen it work either," she responded as Gug and the Bartlett kids made their way around the magician and up the stairs.

Mr. Bartlett's trick may not have worked but theirs sure did. Gug Gazinski was now, at least temporarily, a member of the Bartlett family.

CHAPTER 6
JIMMY FLINT:
PROFESSIONAL SANTA SEEKER

THE NIGHT SHIFT at the New England Division of the North American Aerospace Defense Command (or NORAD as it was called by the military) was quiet as usual. Airman Chester Flint of the United States Air Force watched his section of the sky with heavy eyelids. He knew that, *technically*, calamity could strike at any time and he needed to be ready to defend the free world from asteroids or enemy missiles or whatever else might fall from the heavens.

But the truth was there was nothing happening in the sky on the night of December 17th—same as December 15th and December 14th and every other day during the two years Chester had been stationed at NORAD. So he leaned back in his chair, rested a bag of potato chips on his great big belly and barely kept his drooping eyes on his monitor.

Chester's big brother, Airman First Class Jimmy Flint, was a different story entirely. He was alert at his post, watching three different monitors at once—jotting down notes, reading printouts and reports and comparing data in thick binders. Chester watched Jimmy's intense work for a while before commenting.

"You know, we have a full twelve hour shift, bro. If you don't slow down, you're going to collapse."

Jimmy didn't pay attention. He was engrossed in his work.

"I'm just saying," Chester continued, as he shoved some chips into his mouth, "it's all about pacing. You need to pace yourself ..."

"And you need to be quiet," Jimmy barked. "Just cram some more snacks in your food-hole and shut it. I'm trying to concentrate!"

Chester sank deeper into his chair. He was used to his brother being grouchy most of the time, but that didn't mean he liked it. Chester's eyes landed on the calendar on the wall and then it hit him!

"It's December 17th! That's why you're so uptight today …!"

"*Zip it*," Jimmy snapped, annoyed.

"You're looking for *him*!" Chester shouted.

"I said, *zip it!*" Jimmy repeated.

Chester chuckled, leaned back and filled his mouth with more chips. "Man oh man," he laughed. "Every year, same thing. December 17th and you're looking for Santa Claus like some kind of kid! Ha!"

But at this point, Jimmy wasn't paying attention. He was too busy charting sections of the sky where he thought he might spot Santa—and he had good reason to think it was possible because it was the same area of sky where he had seen Santa exactly nineteen years earlier to the day!

Jimmy was only ten years old at the time and he was staying up late, watching the stars with a telescope when he spotted good old St. Nick. Even though it was midnight, Jimmy could see him clear as day—a great big man in a bright red suit, guiding a glimmering sleigh. He could see the reindeer's fur rustling in the night wind and the moonlight reflecting off the bright whiteness of Santa's beard.

Then, suddenly, as if he knew he was being watched, Santa turned his head in the direction of the telescope and *winked*! He *winked* right at Jimmy! And then with a crack of the reins the reindeer kicked up their legs and the sled shot out of sight in an instant. A moment later, it was as if the sled had never even been there.

Jimmy was ecstatic! He had seen Santa! He ran to the bunk beds he shared with his seven-year-old brother Chester and shook him until he woke up. Jimmy told him what he saw but Chester mumbled that Jimmy must've been dreaming and rolled over and went back to sleep. The next morning Jimmy told his parents at breakfast. They seemed amused but explained that Santa was always careful to not be seen by little boys and girls and, besides, he made his trip around the world on December *24th*, not December *17th*.

What Jimmy's mother and father couldn't have known—*because no one outside of the North Pole knew*—was that Santa *did indeed* fly around the world on December 17th. December 17th was the night of Santa's all-important test run <u>one week before</u> Christmas Eve. He did it just to make sure his flight pattern was all set, the sleigh was operating properly and the reindeer were in tip-top shape.

Jimmy didn't care if anyone believed him. He knew what he saw and he was convinced it meant something special. Santa had *winked* at him! It was as if they had a special connection, *a bond*! He knew, deep in his gut that it was Santa's way of telling him that Christmas that year was going to be the most amazing one ever! And there was only one thing that was going to make that Christmas as special as Jimmy knew it would be—*a Commander Cody Retro Rocket with Optional Bonus Boosters*—the only toy Jimmy had wanted his entire life.

That year, the week from December 17th to Christmas Eve seemed to take forever, but the big night eventually came and Jimmy was so excited he didn't think he'd be able to fall asleep. But he knew he had to, since Santa never gave presents to kids who were awake, so he had taken precautions. He had shoveled the driveway for everyone on the block for free—he wasn't interested in the money, he just wanted to exhaust himself so he'd pass out come bedtime. And at dinner, he poured extra heavy gravy on his Christmas Eve turkey, knowing that a full belly would make him drowsy. By the time he was done with his hot bath that night, he could barely stay awake. He drifted off as soon as he climbed into bed and he dreamt blissfully of his Commander Cody Retro Rocket, guiding it out of Earth's atmosphere, through Saturn's rings, past Pluto and off into the galaxy, searching for adventures unknown.

When morning sunlight came he raced from his bed, not bothering to wake up Chester. He ran down the stairs, two at a time, leaping over the last four steps without even touching them. He searched under the tree for every box he could find with his name on it. He tore the wrapping from each gift in a frenzy and as soon as that present was identified as anything other than a Commander Cody Retro Rocket with Optional Bonus Boosters it was tossed to the side so Jimmy could concentrate on finding the only toy he wanted.

But as the minutes passed and the wrapping paper flew, Jimmy began to get a sick feeling in his stomach. Maybe Santa wasn't bringing him the toy he wanted so badly—the only toy he had *ever* wanted that badly—the only toy he *would* ever want that badly. And then his eyes landed on a box in the corner. It was the right shape. It was the right size. And it had his name on it! The gift-wrap didn't have a chance—it was on the floor in tatters in an instant. Jimmy ripped open the box, shoved his hand inside and pulled out … *a catcher's mitt?*

It couldn't be.

It had to be a mistake.

He had written a letter to Santa telling him what he wanted. And he had been so darn good! Not to mention the fact that Santa had looked right at him and had given him a knowing wink one week earlier!

But Jimmy knew he had opened every gift for him under the tree and none of them was a Commander Cody Retro Rocket.

He turned around, went back upstairs and climbed into bed. And as he lay there, burning with anger, he made himself a promise.

He promised to learn everything he could about astronomy and the study of the sky.

He promised to one-day work at NORAD—which he had learned about at school—where he could use the latest technological advances in astro-surveillance.

He promised that at some point in the future he would be searching the night sky and he would spot that sleigh again—and when he did, he would be ready to finally get his revenge against Santa Claus.

CHAPTER 7
SANTA and ELVIS

IT WAS DARK when Elvis woke up. He had a splitting headache and he could barely lift his head up from the big, fat pillow upon which it was resting. But when he did finally manage to do so, he realized his head hadn't been on top of a pillow. It had been on his boss' stomach.

He had no idea where he was, but he could tell he was in some kind of a convertible sports car. He slowly climbed out and made his way across the room, holding his throbbing head as he blindly searched the wall for a light switch. He found a keypad with buttons and randomly pushed a few until—WHIRRRR—the whole room seemed to come alive with bright fluorescent-esque lights. Elvis squinted, blocking the brightness with his hand.

Once his pupils adjusted, he saw that the room was filled not just with one, but *many*, convertibles. But they didn't look like any cars he'd ever seen—they didn't even have wheels! He looked around and realized that even with the lights on he had no clue as to where they were.

The last thing he remembered was being in Santa's sleigh—as Chief Elf, Elvis got to ride along every year during the December 17th test run. Santa had taken the reindeer to a high altitude to avoid a jet stream of cold air heading their way and in doing so they had to cut through some pretty thick cloud coverage. There was a collision or something—Elvis could remember that much—but that was it. Other than that, he couldn't recall anything!

He hurried to Santa and tried to wake him.

"Hey, Boss!" he said gently tapping Santa's cheeks. "C'mon! Wake up! We gotta figure out where we are and get outta here!"

But Santa was out cold.

Elvis hurried over to the door—at least it looked like a door—but there was no knob. He pushed on it with all his might but it didn't budge. Then he spotted a small, square pad next to the door with no buttons; it was just flat metal. He reached out hesitantly and barely touched it. The door quickly slid open with a *whoosh* sound. Startled, Elvis jumped back.

His heart beating fast, he slowly peeked out into the hall. It didn't look like any hall Elvis had ever seen before. It was dark and curved, and it seemed like if you walked along it, it would take you in a complete circle. Where the curved wall met the ceiling and floor there was faint light that came from a thin tube that ran along the edging and continued, Elvis assumed, all the way around.

"Um, hello?" he called out.

No answer.

"Hey. Anybody out here?" he said a bit louder.

Still no response.

He knew he had to find someone. Santa was still knocked out and there was a chance he needed help. But he couldn't just leave the big guy all alone in that dark garage. So Elvis went back to where Santa was lying and grabbed his boss's ankles. With all his might he pulled Santa from the convertible, causing him to land on the floor with a **thud**. But he still didn't wake up.

"Ooooh. Sorry, Boss!" Elvis said, even though he knew St. Nick couldn't hear him.

He pulled with all his might and, somehow, was able to drag Santa Claus across the floor and to the doorway. This was no small feat considering Santa weighed about 250 pounds more than Elvis.

At the door, Elvis had to catch his breath.

"When … we … get back … to the North Pole," he panted. "You're taking … it easy … with the … eggnog."

Of course Santa didn't respond.

And then, with all his strength mustered, Elvis dragged Santa down the hall, wondering all the time where exactly they were both going and what exactly they would find.

CHAPTER 8
A BRAND NEW TUTU

THEO AND OLIVIA had been arguing for a long time in Theo's room—neither was quite sure how to handle the Gug situation.

"We have to figure out a way to get him back to his family," Olivia pressed.

"The longer we hold onto him, the better the chance some government guys in dark glasses will bust down our door and take us all away to some secret lab! Don't you watch the movies?!" Theo countered.

"Why are you always such a chicken, Theo?"

"I'm not a chicken. I'm making sense."

"Scaredy cat."

"*Am not.*"

"*Are too.* And if you're scared, imagine how frightened *Gug* must be—he's light-years away from his family."

They both turned to Gug who didn't really look too scared at all, actually. He was sitting cross-legged on the window seat with Sophie. They had reached through the open window and were pulling icicles off of the sill and licking them.

"See," Sophie said. "It's nature's ice pop."

Gug licked his icicle, but it stuck to his purplish-grayish tongue. He swung it back and forth, the icicle dangling from the end.

Sophie cackled. So did Gug. When he laughed it sounded like a donkey with laryngitis mixed with an old car engine that wouldn't start.

"Oh yeah," Theo said sarcastically. "He looks *terrified.*"

But Olivia wasn't listening to Theo—she was too busy pulling blankets from his closet.

"What do you think you're doing?" her brother asked.

"Making a bed for Gug," Olivia answered matter-of-factly.

"Not my Star Wars blankets. He'll blow that goop all over them. Give him my race car blanket."

"It's not warm enough. He needs a good night's sleep before school tomorrow."

"*School?! He can't go to school!*" Theo protested.

"What choice do we have?" Olivia countered. "We can't leave him here with Mom all day. *You're* the one who told her Gug was an exchange student. She'll expect him to go to school with us."

"Did you forget about Winston? Gug blasted a snot rocket all over his face. If Winston sees him, he'll kill Gug. And *me*."

"You're always so scared of Winston. He's just an insecure bully."

"Winston's a dillweed! I'm not scared of him ... I'm just scared of *parts* of him. Like his fists," Theo huffed as Gug wandered across the room and picked up Sophie's redheaded, freckle-faced ventriloquist's dummy. He studied it, curious.

"*Ga-gi?*" he asked.

"That's Opie," Sophie explained. "He's my dummy. We're doing the Christmas Pageant Talent Show together. We tell jokes and dance to *Tea For Two*. Here ..."

She took Opie from Gug and positioned the toy on her lap. She moved the dummy's mouth up and down, lowered her voice, and made Opie "talk." Sophie's mouth moved almost as much as Opie's; she wasn't a very good ventriloquist.

"**Hi, Gug. My name's Opie,**" she said in a forced five-year-old baritone.

Gug stared at the talking doll, mesmerized. "*O-peeeeeee,*" he cooed.

The kids all looked at each other, stunned.

"Did you hear that?" Olivia asked in shock.

"He talked!" Sophie exclaimed. "He talked people-talk!" She knelt right in front of Gug and looked him in the eye. "Can you say my name? Can you say Sophie?"

Gug smiled and pointed at her. "Soapy," he said softly.

Sophie beamed. "That's right. I'm Soapy."

"Gug," Olivia said slowly while pointing to herself. "I'm Olivia. I'm going to help you get back home."

"Liv-a" the alien said.

Olivia smiled.

"Don't get too attached guys. He's not staying long," Theo warned.

"Oh don't listen to him," Olivia told Gug. "Theo's a baby."

Gug stepped to Theo and pointed his finger at the boy.

"Tutu," Gug grinned. Olivia and Sophie cracked up.

"No," Theo protested. "Not Tutu. *Theo*."

"Tutu," Gug repeated proud of himself. He pointed to each of them. "Soapy; Liv-a; Tutu."

Theo hung his head, dejected. He knew Tutu was a name his sisters would use long after Gug was gone.

CHAPTER 9
JIMMY PLAYS CONNECT THE DOTS

JIMMY FEVERISHLY POURED through printouts, readouts and reams of data being spit out by rows of computers with more blinking lights than any Christmas tree in all of Millbrook Falls. He checked and rechecked every number, every calculation, every miniscule scrap of information that had been processed at NORAD that night. He knew Santa was up there somewhere, just like he had been when Jimmy was a kid, and there had to be proof of it in the facts and figures covering the more than three thousand pieces of paper Jimmy had printed.

He sat on the floor, surrounded by mounds of documents, furiously scanning each page—highlighting, underlining and cross-referencing. He was so involved in his work that he didn't notice the many paper airplanes Chester had floated his way, each one getting a little bit closer to its intended target—Jimmy's head.

Finally, a nicely crafted glider landed in Jimmy's hair. Jimmy didn't budge. He didn't even acknowledge that something had just become entangled with his chestnut locks. He was simply way too possessed with trying to find proof that Santa was in the sky that night to be bothered by anything else.

Chester stood, throwing his hands up in frustration. "C'mon, bro ... you've been at it for hours and I'm bored! The only big, fat, jolly guy you're gonna find tonight is right here in the room with ya!" he said laughing, shaking his round belly with both hands.

"*Quiet*," Jimmy shushed. "I'm working!"

"You're not working. You're *Santa-hunting*. Like some kind of half crazy nutball." Then a small smile crossed Chester's face. "Speaking of balls, how about I make us a ball and I'll take first shot at the garbage can. Best of out five!"

Chester yanked a sheet from the top of one of Jimmy's paper towers and crumpled it up. Instantly, the tower began to sway a bit ...

"Uh oh," Chester said.

... and then more than a little bit ...

"Oh no!" Jimmy gasped.

... and then it **crashed** to the floor, spewing documents up into the air like a mushroom cloud.

"Chester!" Jimmy shouted. "I had all of these in order!"

"Sorry!" Chester meekly apologized.

"You're always sorry! How about for once, instead of being sorry, you just try to not be an idiot!" Jimmy shouted.

Chester hung his head as he began collecting Jimmy's papers. He knew he messed up—but it was an accident. He had just wanted Jimmy to spend some time with him—*do something fun with him*—but Jimmy never had time for Chester. Not when they were kids. And not now that they were all grown up. And it really hurt Chester sometimes because all he ever wanted for Christmas was for his big brother to like him as much as he liked Jimmy. Heck, he *worshipped* Jimmy—but Jimmy never seemed to notice or care. All he cared about was proving his Santa Claus theory.

"Here ya go," Chester said handing over some of the scattered papers he had collected. Jimmy snatched them from his little brother's hand.

Chester sheepishly grabbed a sky chart that had slid partially under a bookcase. As he handed it over to Jimmy he noticed some readings on it.

"Wow, whole bunch of temperature flares tonight," Chester said like it was no big deal, because to him, it wasn't. "Didn't know we had a meteor shower in the forecast."

Jimmy's head peeked out from under the table where he was gathering some of the papers.

"There wasn't a meteor shower in the forecast. Let me see that readout," he said snatching it away from Chester.

"There had to be," Chester countered with a mouth half-full of chocolate bar he had just bitten into. "We don't get heat flares like that unless metal is moving through the atmosphere at high speed. And the only metal you'll find moving that fast in the sky is iron inside a meteor."

"Wrong!" Jimmy exclaimed as he excitedly used a marker to connect the multiple dots on the readout—each dot indicating one of the heat flares that the NORAD telescope and computer had captured that night. "Tonight is the only other night of the year where you will find _another_ source of metal in the sky! The golden runners of Santa's sleigh! And if you remember from elementary school, gold is an excellent conductor of heat!"

"_For Pete's sake_, Jimmy, would you give up on this Santa thing already! It wasn't him! It wasn't him when you were a kid, and it isn't him showing up on this readout tonight!"

"Really?" Jimmy asked as he spun to Chester with a maniacal look in his eye. "Then how come when I connect the dots representing the locations of the heat flashes, I get … **THIS!**"

Jimmy held up the printout proudly. Chester's jaw dropped open, causing the other half of his candy bar to hit the floor with a thud. He couldn't believe it but right in front of him, right there on the document, was indisputable proof of Jimmy's theory or the greatest coincidence in the history of coincidences!

Because when all the dots representing the location of the various heat-flashes were connected, it created a shape that was _identical to the gold runners and trim of a very large sleigh_!

CHAPTER 10
LET SLEEPING ALIENS LIE!

ELVIS HUFFED AND puffed like the big bad wolf as he pulled a still unconscious Santa down the curving hallways. He had moved Father Christmas at least one hundred yards and they hadn't run into a single other person. They hadn't even come across a staircase or an EXIT sign. Something was wrong—Elvis could feel it in the pit of his stomach, which was jumping with nerves—but he just couldn't figure out what it was.

Just then, he spotted a door! *Thank goodness*, he thought. *Maybe there's someone in there who can tell me how we got here and what the heck is going on!*

He yanked Santa toward the door and pressed his hand against another one of those metal plates that he had seen in the garage where he'd woken up about an hour or so earlier. The door opened up just like the other one had, revealing an eerily dark and quiet room.

"Hi," Elvis whispered. "My name's Elvis. Anyone hear me in there?"

But no one answered. He yanked Santa another foot or so into the room and let go. He collapsed next to Mr. Claus and caught his breath, looking around but unable to see anything in the pitch black.

"Gotta be another one of those light switch pad-thingies by the door somewhere," he said to himself.

And sure enough, after some brief groping, his hands landed on a raised button. He pressed it … and as soon as he did, he immediately wished he hadn't.

Because as soon as the lights went on, Elvis found himself surrounded by a room full of sleeping little green creatures! They were about his height and had long ears that drooped over the sides of their beds. The ends of the ears were shaped kind of like the bellflowers Elvis helped his crazy grandmother plant every spring despite the fact it was still below freezing in the

North Pole at springtime. But at that moment, Elvis was so scared he would've given anything to be back at his grandmother's garden, shivering in the cold, haplessly planting seeds in the ice with nutty old Grandma.

But instead, he was in a room surrounded by what looked like aliens, outnumbered nine to two. Well, actually he was outnumbered nine to *one* because his employer, Santa Claus, was still not awake … however, one of the little green guys *was*.

Elvis heard him rustling around in his wall-mounted semi-circular bed. The beds were stacked five high on opposite sides of the room—the lowest beds just a foot off the ground, the highest beds several feet from the floor. One of the beds was empty. Elvis had no way of knowing that the party that was supposed to be occupying that bed was currently asleep in Millbrook Falls, New Hampshire.

Elvis turned toward the sound to find what appeared to be a sleepy and confused critter rubbing his eyes and blinking as he got accustomed to the light. But soon his eyes adjusted and they locked onto Elvis. Elvis was about to say something to reassure the creature that he meant no harm but he had barely opened his mouth when …

Guuuuugggggghhhhh! The alien screeched as loud as he could, pointing to the intruder and his partner in the strange red costume.

Green gunk flew *everywhere*, but mostly onto Elvis.

"No, no, don't yell!" Elvis pleaded. But then another alien, hearing the cries, woke up and, seeing Elvis, screamed as well! And then another awoke! And then another! Soon they were all spraying goop and wailing away—the noise was loud enough to even wake Santa who sat up, totally perplexed.

"Elvis," Santa stammered wide-eyed. "What in the name of Christmas is going on here?"

Elvis began backing toward the door as he had noticed the little beings begin to climb out of their beds and slowly move toward them. They were all pointing to the empty wall-mounted bed and it seemed to disturb them quite a bit.

"Not sure boss. But if I were you, I'd get ready to …"

One of the aliens pointed at Elvis and Santa and shouted … *"Goo-gaaaaaaaaaaaa!"*

"... *Run!!*" Elvis cried out, finishing his sentence as he and Santa sprinted from the room and down the curved hallway, a gang of nine very angry aliens on their heels. They all wanted to know who these strangers were, why they were on their spaceship and what they had done with their brother!

CHAPTER 11

DON'T GET CAUGHT IN THE MALL
IN YOUR UNDERWEAR!

"GET DOWN ON the ground and put your hands on top of your head!" the police officer shouted.

Artie Sneed hit the floor as fast as he could and put his hands on his head, just like he was told. He knew he was in trouble. It's bad enough getting caught in the mall at 3 AM—five hours after it has closed ... but it's even worse when you get caught in just a t-shirt and your underwear.

Two police officers raced over and began to handcuff Artie.

"Please, I can explain. I'm Santa Claus," he stammered.

"Sure you are, pal," one of the cops said. "And I'm the Queen of England."

"I knew you were trouble when I hired you!" Mr. Lipson spit-shouted, as he appeared from the shadows of the darkened mall. "Look at you—robbing my mall in the middle of the night—in your underwear no less! And we don't even sell that brand of underwear! Where's your mall loyalty, Sneed?!"

"But, Mr. Lipson," Artie begged. "I'm not robbing the mall. I swear!"

"Of course you're not," Lipson answered sarcastically. "You're just practicing to become one of our lingerie models! Take him away, officers!"

"No, wait," Sneed pleaded. "I can tell you what happened! It's all a mistake!"

Artie quickly explained how he had spent hours on end the night before listening to the Christmas wishes of every little brat in town and how he had almost wrapped up for the night when the last kid on his lap threw up all over him.

He yelled at the punk and as the child's mother took the crying toddler away, Artie stormed into the Millbrook Falls Mall Employee Locker Room and threw his Santa suit in the beat up washer/dryer they kept back there. The washer was only supposed to be used for the janitor's uniforms but Artie had worn only the Santa suit to the mall and wasn't about to drive home smelling like some kid's puke.

So while his clothes were being cleaned, Artie realized he was famished. But he couldn't go out to the food court in his t-shirt and underwear, so he decided to raid the employee's refrigerator. He found a huge turkey and cheese sub sandwich with extra pickles and mayo.

"That was my sandwich!" Lipson shouted. "My wife made that for me! I was saving it for tomorrow!"

"Well, tell her it was delicious," Artie said sheepishly. He continued on that after his big meal and a long workday, he decided to lie down on the old couch in the corner. He dozed off and slept through the night while the mall was shut down. He woke up about twenty minutes ago and realized not only that he was locked inside the mall until morning but that he was very thirsty. So he headed out in search of a water fountain since the locker room fridge only had iced tea and he hated iced tea.

He got a drink and was heading back to the locker room when he heard the police tell him to drop to the ground.

"And then here we are," Sneed finished up. "I swear that's the truth. Check the fridge if you want—you'll see, the sub sandwich is gone. And look at me! I don't have any money or stolen jewelry on me. And besides, who robs a store in his underwear?!"

The police looked at Sneed and then at Mr. Lipson.

"His story does seem to make sense," one officer said.

After a moment, Mr. Lipson agreed, "I guess so."

"Ok," the other officer said as he uncuffed Artie. "Then we're done here. But when your employee tripped the silent motion detector alarm in the mall, since he wasn't really robbing anything, it was a *false alarm*. And under the new laws passed by the town council, every time the police are forced to respond to a *false alarm* there is a five hundred dollar fine. You'll be getting the bill within the week, Mr. Lipson."

Mr. Lipson could not contain his rage.

"You moron!" he shouted at Artie as they police left the mall. "That five hundred dollar fine is coming out of your pay!"

"But I don't even make five hundred dollars."

"Then you'll work for free for the rest of the holiday season!"

"Listen to me," Artie growled. "I can barely pay the rent for my lousy apartment as it is! I'm flat broke! You can't make me work for free!"

"I can and I will," Lipson shot back. "Until every penny of the five hundred dollar fine is paid back! And if you don't, I will sue you in court! Now get some clothes on and get out of my mall!"

Artie stood there alone, in the dark, in his underwear, and watched his boss leave.

And as Mr. Lipson reached the end of the hallway, he turned back and shouted, "And you're replacing that turkey sub, too!" And then he slammed the door behind him.

CHAPTER 12
THE NEW KID IN SCHOOL

THEO WAS A nervous wreck walking to school the next morning. He kept readjusting Gug's scarf around his face, making sure it wouldn't slip and reveal the alien that was underneath all the layers.

"Stop messing with it," Olivia counseled.

"You want it to fall off?" Theo countered. "So then everyone can see our little pal here?"

"He's covered from head to toe. No one will see him."

"Yeah, head to toe," Sophie parroted. "I like his clothes. You look so handsome, Gug!"

Theo couldn't really argue with his sisters. They had dressed Gug in a puffy, down ski jacket; jeans; boots; a hunting cap with earflaps; gloves and sunglasses.

"No one will be able to tell, Theo. Don't worry about it so much," Olivia added.

"Yeah, well, here comes the first test," Theo said, pointing to his best friend, Felix, who was crossing the street toward them.

"What's up, butt-brains?!" Felix shouted because Felix shouted basically everything. He was a freckle-faced, heavy-set kid who didn't have an OFF switch. He was loud and energetic and inappropriate a lot of the time, but he was also loyal and honest and that's why he had been Theo's best friend since first grade.

"Hey, Felix," Theo greeted.

"Who's this guy?" Felix said taking in Gug in his crazy get-up.

"This is Gug. Exchange student. We're taking him in for a while."

"Since when?" Felix asked. "You never said anything about an exchange student."

"I don't know. Since whenever. I don't have to tell you everything I'm doing," Theo responded.

"What's with the outfit?" Felix wanted to know. "It's not like it's a hundred below. Hey, kid, you speak English or something?"

"Actually he doesn't," Olivia answered. "And he's from ... Ghana—where it's very hot—so he's not used to the cold. So he'll have to be bundled up all the time—even inside—or his blood could freeze."

"I thought he was from Iceland," Sophie blurted.

"No," Olivia said looking at Sophie in a way that said *shut up and follow my lead.* "He's from Ghana. That's where he comes from."

Gug pointed at the sky. "Come from ..." he repeated.

Felix snorted a laugh. "Someone needs to get this kook a map. Well, smell ya later in math class, dingleberry!" and he ran off to the school across the street.

Theo exhaled. "Man, if we can barely trick Felix, how are we going to trick the teachers?" he asked.

"Very carefully," was Olivia's answer.

But as it turned out, fooling the teachers wasn't that difficult. Since Gug was pretending to be a twelve-year-old like Theo; that put him in the sixth grade which meant he had different teachers for different subjects instead of one teacher all day. And since each teacher only had to have Gug as an extra student for one forty-five minute class per day, none of them really paid too much mind to the boy from Ghana. They all bought that he didn't speak too much English—though Gug was picking up words and expressions at an amazing rate—and they didn't fight Theo's claim that Gug had to wear the extra clothes inside the school because, being from the African nation of Ghana, he was having a great deal of trouble adjusting to the cold of New Hampshire. Most teachers were afraid of being labeled culturally insensitive if they made Gug take off his layers.

In science class, Mr. Wickman did demand that Gug at least take his sunglasses off. "I like to see whom I'm talking to," he insisted. "And besides, it's not like his *eyes* are going to freeze."

Theo had no choice. He motioned to Gug to remove his sunglasses and Gug did. Luckily, between the pulled-down hat, the wrapped-high scarf, the jacket collar and the earflaps, all you could see were Gug's eyes and nothing else. They were getting away with it!

But one class where Theo *knew* they couldn't get away with it was gym. In gym, Gug would have to wear shorts and a t-shirt and then that would be the end of them all! So Theo tracked down Olivia in between classes and said she had to take over the baby-sitting for a while.

"But I have home economics," Olivia pointed out. "It's the one elective class fourth graders are allowed to take. If I mess things up I'll never be able to take a big-kid class again!"

"Why are you always such a nerd?" Theo barked. "It's just for one class. Bake some cookies with him and then I'll take him to play rehearsal, okay? What could go wrong?"

"Fine," Olivia huffed. "C'mon, Gug." But when she turned, Gug wasn't there. "Where'd he go?!"

They both scanned the crowded hallway.

"Oh no!" Theo gasped, spotting Gug at the water fountain. He had turned the handle and was touching the water stream with his finger, somehow *freezing* the water in mid-air! Then he snapped off the icicle and licked it, just like he had done with Sophie the night before at the windowsill.

Theo grabbed Gug and directed him away from the water fountain before anyone could see what the alien was doing.

"Soapy," Gug said, holding up the newly formed icicle.

"Yes, you can give that to Soapy later, okay?"

"Tutu?" Gug said, offering the icicle to Theo after taking his own lick with his purplish-grayish tongue, leaving a small trail of slime behind. Theo, totally grossed out, made a face and gently pushed the offering away.

"*Tutu?!*" Gug said louder pushing the icicle back at Theo. "Lick lick."

"No. No lick lick," Theo protested.

"Just lick the darn thing, Tutu," Olivia hissed, "before he makes a scene!"

"Fine," Theo spat, snatching the icicle from Gug. He took it, scrunched up his face in disgust and licked where the alien had licked, slime and all.

"Ugh," Theo said, grossed-out.

"*Gug,*" the alien corrected.

CHAPTER 13

SUGAR RUSH

THINGS STARTED OUT smoothly enough in Home Economics class. Mrs. Fink, the teacher, was excited to have Gug sit in on their session since it was not very often that boys took that class.

They were making cookies that day and Gug loved watching Olivia mix and measure, stir and pour. He was mesmerized by all of the equipment and tools used in the baking process and he sat quietly and watched. Olivia even let him hold the electric batter mixer.

And that was the beginning of the end, because as Gug moved the mixer around in the bowl some of the batter splattered on his gloves.

"Oh, I'll get you a paper towel to clean that up," Olivia offered. But when she turned to the kitchen counter top, Gug, curious, extended his purplish-grayish tongue and licked the icing off. It instantly sent shock waves through Gug's entire body—but mostly to his brain—and mostly to the part of his brain that said, *'That was fantastic! Now give me some more of whatever that was!"*

Gug had never had sugar before and it was love at first taste! But it seems that sugar is absorbed and metabolized a lot differently by aliens than it is by humans. Where sugar might make a regular kid a little hyper, it makes alien kids go out of their minds!

By the time Olivia turned around Gug was devouring an entire plate of brownies the previous class had made! He was shoving them in so fast that crumbs and brownie pieces were flying everywhere!

"Gug! Stop that this instant!" Mrs. Fink shouted. But Gug didn't hear her. Or, more accurately, he *heard* her but he didn't process what she was saying because he was too focused on the tray of chocolate-cluster-nut-bars he had just spotted.

"*Goooooooo*," Gug cooed softly as his eyes landed on the gooey, nutty treats.

"*No!*" Olivia said diving for Gug but she was too late. He leapt up onto the long baking table and ran across it toward the goodies, knocking over milk and stepping in mixing bowls of icing along the way. Ingredients flew behind him like the back wheels of a car kicking up mud in a wet field—and they all seemed to splatter across Olivia's face as she chased after him.

He stepped on the edge of large serving platter, causing the other side of the plate to pop upward like a teeter-totter. This sent several eggs soaring through the air, two of which landed right in Mrs. Fink's hair!

"Someone stop him!" Mrs. Finks bellowed as egg yolk dripped down her face. But the other children just backed away from what they thought was a sugar-crazed student.

Gug got to the nut clusters and practically poured the entire contents of the tray right into his mouth, barely chewing and basically swallowing them whole. Olivia lunged for Gug but he dodged her advance and she landed face-first in a pile of flour!

He ducked and ran between the legs of an approaching Mrs. Fink and made it to the other side of the room where a tin of cream puffs sat on the teacher's desk. The puffs had no chance. Gug shoved them in his mouth as fast as he could—making them disappear as if they were nothing but tiny mints, as opposed to fairly large pastries. Within a matter of seconds the tin was empty!

Gug spun around to see what other sugary goodness awaited him but a very stern-looking Mrs. Fink grabbed him by the shoulders.

"That is *enough* young man," she scolded. She stared into the sugar-crazed eyes of a heavy-breathing Gug. His scarf and hat and clothes were covered in confectioner's sugar and cupcake sprinkles. "I don't know if this is how children act in Home Economics in Ghana, but it is not how we do things in Millbrook Falls."

Luckily the bell sounded, signifying the end of class. Mrs. Fink wiped egg from her forehead and looked at the second oldest Bartlett child.

"Olivia," the teacher said calmly, trying to regain her composure. "I do not think home economics is the right class for your friend. And as for today's project—you will both receive an F."

Olivia's eyes welled up—she had never gotten anything below an *A minus* before in her life. But she knew better than to argue so she just nodded and led Gug toward the door. On the way out he noticed cookies on a table and reached for them.

"Cook-a-goo."

"Don't even think about it," Olivia grunted, knocking them out of his hand as she moved him out the door.

CHAPTER 14
LIGHTS! CAMERA! DISASTER!

"WHAT HAPPENED TO you?!" Theo asked when he saw Olivia, covered in more icing and flour than a birthday cake. "And how did he get so messy?"

"Don't ask," Olivia answered.

Gug was still a little hyper, bouncing gently on the balls of his feet.

"Gug like cook-a-goo. Tutu like cook-a-goo?"

"Cook-a-goo?" Theo wondered aloud.

"Cookie." Olivia explained. "And he can't have any. *Ever*. He doesn't do well with sugar."

"Sugar. Gug like sugar," their little alien friend panted.

"I can't believe how fast he's learning our language," Theo marveled.

"*I* can't believe he just made me get my first F. In home economics! The easiest of the *easy A's* and I got an *F*," Olivia muttered as she walked off.

Theo looked to Gug. "I have play rehearsal now. And I don't want you messing it up like you did in Home Ec? Ok?"

"Ok, Tutu," Gug answered, following Theo down the hall and into the school auditorium.

Mr. Greene, the drama teacher, was already working with NOEL—a student band made up of twins Lee and Matthew Chong on bass and guitar, sixth grader Scott Kolbrenner on drums and Kenny Sklar on vocals. They were doing their own version of "Jingle Bell Rock" and it was pretty good except for the fact that Scott Kolbrenner wore a ridiculous red jacket with zippers covering every inch of it.

Theo and Gug headed backstage where Felix was working. He and Theo were stagehands—responsible for lowering and raising the curtains, changing the lights and switching out the props. Felix did it because he liked all the buttons and levers and switches he got to operate. Theo liked it because he had the best seat in the house to watch Lisa Connelly.

Theo had been is school with Lisa Connelly since kindergarten. She had long brown hair, brown eyes and the voice of an angel. He had never said more than "hello" to her or "have a good day" or "see you next fall" at the end of the school year. She was always polite, but Theo was pretty certain that—at least in Lisa Connelly's eyes—he didn't exist. Theo thought about that fact for a moment—Gug, *an alien from another planet*, existed, but somehow Theo didn't—at least not to the girl he'd had a crush on since he could remember.

Felix saw Theo and Gug approaching. "Hey, Theo. You're late."

"Sorry. Had to get Gug. He wants to help us out."

"Cool," Felix said. "And don't worry, you didn't miss her."

"Huh? Who?" Theo said trying to sound casual.

"Please. Don't try to pretend you're not doing this only to be around Lisa."

"Shhhh," Theo hushed. "Someone might hear."

"Lisa?" Gug asked.

"Yup," Felix answered. "Theo loves Lisa. Speaking of which, she's on now."

Theo turned to see Lisa and four other seventh grade girls walk onto the stage in red dresses with white puffy trim. They got in position with Lisa in the middle, flanked by two girls on either side. From the side stage area, Felix turned on some lights that made Christmas colors of red and white shine on the performers.

"Use a little blue," Theo said wistfully, never taking his eyes off Lisa. "It makes her look like an angel."

"Oh brother," Felix groaned. But he shined a blue light on stage as well just to make his best friend happy.

The music started and the girls began their routine, singing "Santa Baby". There were five girls on the stage but as far as Theo was concerned there might as well have only been one because all he saw was Lisa.

But Gug, unfortunately, saw something else entirely. He saw something coming down from the rafters above the stage … and it was terrible. Well, at least it was terrible to Gug.

In reality it wasn't that bad at all—it was just part of the production. About a minute into the song, Felix was supposed to lower a large plastic statue of Santa from the ceiling onto the stage and Lisa and the girls would dance around it and sing.

But to Gug, this statue wasn't a loveable symbol of Christmas.

To Gug, it was the guy who smashed into his Starhopper—a small disc-like mini-flying saucer that alien kids used for fun. In fact, it was inside that very Starhopper that Elvis found himself when he woke up in the garage of the mothership spacecraft.

Seeing Santa coming down from the rafters made Gug remember everything in a flash. His parents were using a transporter beam to zap him and his 9 brothers and sisters back into the cargo hold of the mothership because, like most kids, they weren't listening when their parents announced over the spaceship's exterior speakers that it was time to come inside. As Gug watched his brother Zned and his sister Xnaxgard disappear before his eyes and get transported away from all the fun they were having, Gug decided to hide from his parents' technological reach.

He saw a cloud bank up ahead and he raced there as quickly as he could, putting the Starhopper into overdrive and making it go over 100 glopnars per hour. But when he turned behind the clouds a massive sleigh pulled by strange creatures barreled into him. The only thing he remembers after that was flying through the air, landing in a big sack and then crashing to the ground. Then, Liv-a, Soapy and Tutu found him.

He missed his mommy and his daddy and his brothers and sisters. And it was all the fault of the man coming down from the ceiling in the auditorium! It was all the fault of the man in the red suit! Gug was so filled with rage! And ANGER! And **FURY**!!!

"Guuuuuuuuuuuuuuuuuuug!" he shouted as he raced onto the stage!

"Gug! No!" Theo called but Gug had already leaped into the air and landed onto the Santa statue, wrapping his arms and legs around it like a monkey!

Lisa and the girls *shrieked* as the statute swung back and forth across the stage with Gug clinging to it, beating on Santa with all his might—furious at the man who took him away from his family!

"Get him off of there!" Mr. Greene shouted.

"I'm trying!" Theo said, jumping up to grab Gug—but he just missed by inches each time. Theo realized Felix was yanking on the rope, causing the statute to move up and down in addition to back and forth.

"*What the heck are you doing?!*" Theo shouted.

"Trying to shake him loose!" Felix shouted back.

"Well stop! He's not a piñata!"

"Ok," Felix said, and he let go of the rope. Gug and the statue came *crashing* to the ground. The statue broke into several pieces.

Gug stood up and looked at the statue, confused—and a little scared. He thought he had killed the man in the red suit.

"It's not real, Gug," Theo whispered.

"No real?" Gug said, poking Santa's head with his foot.

"Ok! That's it! Have you boys lost your minds?!" Mr. Greene said storming onto the stage.

"No, sir, it's just—" Theo tried to explain but the drama teacher cut him off.

"—I want you and Felix and … and I don't even know who this other kid is …"

"Gug," Gug offered.

"… And *Goog* here," Mr. Greene continued, "… *off my stage this instant!* You are suspended from the play for the rest of the week! And consider yourselves lucky I'm not throwing you out of the production entirely!"

Theo, Felix and Gug dejectedly walked off the stage. When they passed Lisa, Theo looked at her. All he could say was "Sorry."

Gug picked up on the sadness and defeat in Theo's voice.

As they exited the auditorium, Gug reached up and took hold of Theo's hand. Gug knew he had messed things up for his human friend. He didn't know enough of their language to fully express how badly he felt, but he was smart enough to understand the meaning of the word Theo had just used. So he decided to use it as well.

"Gug sorry too, Tutu."

But Theo didn't say anything back. He was beginning to feel he should've fought his sisters harder when he said he wanted to leave Gug back in the woods where they found him.

CHAPTER 15

THE SHORTEST CHAPTER
IN THE BOOK

"PACK YOUR THINGS! We're leaving!" Jimmy Flint shouted, jolting Chester awake and making his brother fall out of his workstation chair.

Chester rubbed his eyes, blinking them open to find Jimmy hurriedly collecting his papers and shoving them into a folder.

"What's going on?" Chester asked, still half-asleep.

"Well, while you were _snoring_ away, dear brother, I was _working_ away."

"Good, because I was out cold; I haven't checked the monitors in hours—"

"—I wasn't working on _work_," Jimmy scoffed. "I was working on getting Santa. I've calculated the trajectory of Santa's sleigh's descent toward earth, the approximate speed at which he must have been going, the estimated weight of the sleigh based on the measurements of the heat flares—I know where he landed! I figured it out!"

"Are you sure?" Chester asked.

"As sure as I am that a catcher's mitt makes a lousy Christmas gift," Jimmy responded as he pulled on his winter jacket. "So grab your hat and coat and sack of snacks and whatever else you need because you and I are about to take a trip to a little town called Millbrook Falls!"

CHAPTER 16

DISORDER IN THE COURT!

"I'M TELLING YOU, I'm Santa Claus! Haven't any of you ever heard of me?!" Santa shouted.

"For the last time," Elvis grumped, "they can't understand you! And stop shouting; you're an inch from my ear."

Elvis struggled against the netting that had both he and Santa bound up tight. He was still frustrated that they had been caught. They had outrun the creatures that had chased them and had given them the slip by climbing into some kind of ventilation duct in one of the side hallways. But the vent was on a downward slope, and gravity isn't a friend to a three hundred pound guy in a slick velvet suit. So once Santa started to slide down the duct, he smashed into Elvis—who had entered before him—and they both rocketed about one hundred feet until they crashed through another vent (this one in the ceiling) and landed in a heap on the floor.

When they looked up, they found two much larger green creatures looking down at them. One of them—the one that had fuller lips and more almond-shaped eyes—let out a shriek. The other one pointed a weapon at them—it turned out to be some kind of webbing shooter and it fired upon Santa and Elvis the thick, silky ropes that they now found themselves tangled up in.

After that, most of it was a blur. The full-lipped creature kept shrieking and shouting gibberish at them (*Goog-a-goog!! Gaga-laga-baga-boo!!*), while the larger one pressed some controls on a panel that seemed to have a thousand buttons. About fifteen minutes later a bunch of greenies with their own weapons came rushing into the room. They helped Elvis and Santa to their feet and shuttled them out into a small hallway that connected to another, smaller ship. That ship had a cage in it—it looked suspiciously like a jail cell—and Elvis began to worry that they were in the custody of some kind of space police!

After a short ride in the smaller craft, they were led out of the ship and into a building. Santa only got a quick glimpse when they were being transferred, but he could have sworn the building was floating—it seemed to hover just a few feet off the ground!

When Santa and Elvis got inside they were forced to stand on a platform. Once they were both on it, one of the space cops pressed a button on a remote control and a buzzing force field surrounded them. Santa instinctively stepped back from the buzzing, accidentally pressing his backside into the force field behind him.

"Eeeeeow!" he cried, rubbing his butt with his white-gloved hand. "That smarts!"

"Guess we're stuck in here," Elvis muttered.

Sitting in seats high above them, seven aliens in capes looked down at the captives. The creatures looked like judges overseeing a court. Elvis was now no longer worried that they were in the custody of space police—he knew that they were in the custody of space police. And even worse, he and Santa seemed to be on trial!

CHAPTER 17
MAKING A BREAK FOR IT!

THEO PACED BACK and forth in his room, addressing his sisters and Gug.

"This was a mistake from the beginning!" he stressed. "I never wanted to bring him here and I sure as heck didn't want to bring him to school!"

"You're being mean to our guest," Sophie scolded, putting her hand on Gug's. Gug looked sad—he felt terrible about how things went at Eisenhower Memorial.

"Mean? Do you know what he did today? He humiliated me in front of Lisa!"

"Tutu love Lisa," Gug said, hoping that talk of Lisa and Theo's love for her would cheer up his friend.

It didn't.

"Oh be quiet," Theo snapped.

"And I got an F today. And that's going to throw off my entire report card, Gug," Olivia added, also mad at their guest.

Sophie put her arm around Gug protectively.

"Stop it you guys," she said. "You're not being nice." She turned to Gug, "It's okay. They're just cranky. I get like that if I don't nap."

"I'm not cranky," Theo said. "I'm worried. I'm worried about how long we can keep *an alien* living with us before someone finds out. I'm worried about what happens tomorrow when we bring him back to school—"

"*I'm* worried about how we're going to save Christmas! Have we forgotten about that?!" Olivia added. "It's less than a week away and we have no idea where in the universe Santa has wound up! Or do you still believe that sleigh is from the *mall*, Theo?"

Theo couldn't deny it any longer. Not after the way Gug reacted when he saw the Santa statue at rehearsal. The alien had clearly seen Santa before and had some kind of mishap with him. Theo just had to admit it—Santa Claus was real. But worse, he was *missing and most likely in trouble*!

Thud—thud—thud.

The knocking at Theo's bedroom door made them all freeze. "Kids," their father called, "open up. I've got something to show you."

"*And now*," Theo whispered, his eyes wide with anxiety, "*I'm worried that our dad is right outside our door!*"

Olivia sprung up and ushered Sophie and Gug into the bathroom that connected Theo's room to hers.

"Don't make a sound," she stressed to her sister.

"You owe Gug an apology—" Sophie protested but Olivia just pushed them into the bathroom and slammed the door shut. She gave the *all-clear* sign to Theo who took a deep breath and opened his bedroom door. Mr. Bartlett barged right in, very excited.

"Ok, guys, you ready to be amazed?" he said. "Hey, where's Sophie? She should see this trick."

"She's in the bathroom," Olivia explained.

"Oh. I'll just wait for her," their dad offered.

"Um … it might be a while," Theo explained. "Franks 'n beans for lunch at school today."

"Ohhhhh," Mr. Bartlett nodded knowingly.

"Besides," Olivia added with fake enthusiasm. "We really wanna see the trick *now*."

"Yeah," Theo agreed, following his sister's lead. "We really wanna see it, Dad."

"Ok, you got it!" Mr. Bartlett said, feeding off of the kids' energy. He raised his hands high in the air. "Lady and Gentleman," he called out. "I present to you, for your amazement and pleasure … THE GREAT GOODBYE!"

Oh no, the kids thought. *Here we go again.*

Mr. Bartlett whipped his arms down with gusto!

… And once again, nothing happened. Just two little smoke pellets fell from his sleeves and landed on the ground at his children's feet.

"Um ... maybe it's a good idea Sophie didn't see this. Guess I still don't have all the kinks worked out," their father said embarrassed.

"That's ok, Dad," Olivia said. "You keep at it and come show us when you're ready."

Mr. Bartlett nodded and left the room defeated.

Theo closed the door behind him and hurried to the bathroom.

"Ok, guys," he said as he opened the door. "You can come out now–"

But when Theo entered the bathroom, no one was in there. But the window was open, the curtain blowing in the cold December breeze.

"Look!" Olivia said pointing next to the sink.

Theo spun to see what his sister had discovered. It was a message written on the counter top tile in bright blue toothpaste: **You were mean. We ran away. (p.s. U guys stink)**

CHAPTER 18
A BRIGHT IDEA

SOPHIE AND GUG dragged a small suitcase behind them—each of them holding on to the handle with one hand—as they made their way down Main Street through a light snow that silently fell throughout all of Millbrook Falls. Gug was dressed as any kid would be during a New Hampshire winter, so he wasn't recognizable as an alien underneath his winter garb. And though he and Sophie were pretty young to be out at night on their own, the adults in town were so busy doing last minute Christmas shopping that they hardly noticed the five-year-old and her pal from outer space.

"Don't worry, Gug," Sophie huffed as she trudged through the snow-covered sidewalks. "We'll go somewhere where we're appreciated."

"Gug go to school?" Gug asked.

"No, not school. That didn't work out so well," Sophie answered.

"Gug go back Soapy's house?"

"No," Sophie answered. "We're not wanted there."

Gug walked alongside the little girl for a silent moment. Then he stopped and looked at her with sad eyes. He pointed toward the heavens.

"Gug go Momma?" he asked softly.

Sophie felt so bad for her friend.

"I don't know how to get you there," Sophie answered. "I'm sorry." She hated saying that to him, but she had to tell him the truth.

But Gug wasn't paying much attention to Sophie at this point. He was looking past her, to the window display of *Bosley's Electronics and Appliance Store*. There were several TVs in the display and all of them were tuned to the same show—*Rudolph The Red Nosed Reindeer*. But Gug wasn't focused on Rudolph—he was staring at the movie's cartoon figure of Santa Claus.

Sophie quickly saw the alien's eyes shift from sadness to anger in an instant.

"*Santa*," Gug said with a quiet intensity.

"Um ... are you okay, Gug?" Sophie asked warily.

"Santa!" Gug said a little louder, rage filling his voice.

"Uh ... Gug?"

"SANTA!!!" Gug shouted as he charged the display window and began pounding on the three-inch-thick glass with all his might. He was still so angry with the man in the red suit. It was his fault that Gug was away from his family, from his brothers and sisters, from his mom and dad. And everywhere he looked he saw this big, red Santa-man ... in the sky, in the school auditorium and now on the earthling's talking-picture-screens!

Sophie pulled Gug, manic and furious, away from the window.

"Stop! People are looking—they might figure out what you really are!" she said quietly but forcefully in his ear.

Gug looked at her with wild eyes, panting.

"Santa smash Gug ... Santa send Gug here ... Santa take Gug from family."

"Gug," Sophie said calmly, trying to soothe him. "Is that what happened? Santa's sleigh smashed into your spaceship?"

Gug nodded.

"That's called an *accident*. It means *not on purpose*."

"Accident?" Gug asked.

"Yeah. Like you had in cooking class. And play rehearsal. Santa's good. He gives presents. Makes kids happy. He didn't mean to smash into you."

Gug turned back to the display window—a commercial was playing on all the TV screens now. In it, Santa handed two little kids presents next to a Christmas tree. Realization filled Gug's eyes.

"Santa good," he said softly. "Accident. Like Gug."

Sophie could tell from the tone of Gug's voice that he understood now.

"C'mon," she said. "We should get to the bus station. I'm thinking Las Vegas—my Uncle Phil taught me how to play blackjack. We should be okay."

"Ok, Soapy," Gug said as they continued on their way.

"Sophie! Gug! Wait!" a voice cried out behind them. Gug and Sophie both turned to see ...

"Tutu!" Gug cried happily. "Liv-a!"

Theo and Olivia were racing across Veteran's Square—past the gazebo and the swing sets—right toward them. They were both incredibly worried.

"What are you guys doing?" Theo shouted as he reached his sister and the alien. "You can't just run away!"

"Can too!" Sophie shot back. "I have four dollars. So we can buy food and a house and we won't have to live with you guys any more!"

Olivia knelt in the snow so she could be eye level with Sophie and Gug.

"Guys, we're sorry we were so unkind. We were upset, but we didn't mean it," she said.

"Accident," Gug said matter-of-factly. "Not on purpose."

"That's right," Theo said. "It wasn't on purpose that we were mean. We were just dillweeds."

"No. *Winston's* a dillweed," Gug corrected, remembering what he had heard about the town bully from Theo himself.

Theo and Olivia both laughed. But Sophie did not. Olivia noticed.

"What's wrong?" she asked her kid sister. "You still angry?"

"No," Sophie said sadly. "It's just ... Gug wants to go home. He misses his family. Imagine if you got separated from your family —would you be happy?"

Theo and Olivia thought about that. Maybe a couple of days ago Theo would have said that he'd <u>love</u> to be separated from his annoying sisters. But since they'd met Gug—since they'd all been working together as a team—he had to admit to himself that maybe he'd miss them a little bit. But he'd never admit that to Olivia and Sophie! And though Olivia was having a similar thought, she would never confess it to her siblings either!

"But we have no way of getting him home," Sophie continued. "We have no way to help him ..."

Sophie trailed off. Her voice caught in her throat and her eyes welled up. She was almost about to cry but didn't want to. She wanted to be tough.

Gug put his hand on her shoulder.

"No sad, Soapy," he said.

"We'll think of something," Theo said, but he didn't sound convincing. "We'll figure out a way to get you up back up there."

"No we won't," Olivia said, a sudden strength to her voice.

"Hey, I know that," Theo whispered. "I'm just trying to make them feel better—"

"—No," Olivia interrupted, her eyes glued to Mr. Ferro's Christmas Tree Lot across the street from them—more particularly, she was focused on the two massive spotlights that Mr. Ferro shone up into the night sky to draw attention to his business. "I don't mean we can't get Gug home. We just can't get Gug **_back up there_**. But we just might be able to get his family to come get him **_down here!_**"

CHAPTER 19
A PLAN PUT INTO ACTION!

OLIVIA'S PLAN WAS complicated and confusing and contained a lot of math and geometry and Theo couldn't follow it at all.

"I don't get it," he said, pacing back and forth in the Bartlett's' garage. "How is this going to work?"

Olivia took a deep breath and exhaled. She was much better in school than Theo and she sometimes got frustrated when she had to explain things to him over and over again. Normally she would've just yelled at him and called him a dummy, but she could see he was trying really hard to understand so she gathered herself and started over.

She took a piece of chalk from Gug who was out of his bundles of clothing and sitting on a large log of rolled-up carpet with Sophie. Olivia had to pull the chalk from his mouth because he was sucking on it. She approached the L'il Artist blackboard that Sophie had gotten for her last birthday. She used the chalk to point to sketches she had already drawn.

"Okay. Santa's sleigh was found here in the woods, right?" she said patiently, pointing to a crude drawing of a sled.

"Yup. I understand that much," Theo said.

"And the sleigh tracks in the snow," she said. "They were about thirty feet or so long. It's just an estimate but an estimate is all we need. So if we can figure out the acute angle at which the sleigh approached the woods ..."

Theo was already starting to get confused.

"And measure the speed of impact ..."

Theo's head was starting to hurt from thinking too much.

"And then do a reverse triangulation computation ..." At this point Olivia was writing algebraic and geometric calculations and notations all over the blackboard. Theo was lost, but he didn't snap at Olivia as he usually would have. He could tell she was being understanding with him and he appreciated it. He may have always made fun of Olivia for caring so much about her schoolwork, but the truth was, he was secretly a little envious—she was smart as heck and he was really impressed that she could figure all this stuff out.

"… And so that would give us the approximate point of impact in the sky between Gug and Santa's sleigh. Then all we'd have to do is shine a signal up into the night sky at that location and hope Gug's family sees it."

"But they could be miles away from where the accident was," Theo pointed out. "*Light-years* away."

"They have to know he's missing by now," Sophie said, opening a bag of cookies from a supply shelf where the Bartletts stored food and snacks. "They'll go back to where they last saw him. Like that time when I left Opie in the park." She popped a cookie in her mouth and then pressed play on CD player. "Tea for Two" played and Sophie stood up and did a dance with Opie.

"Not the best time for dancing, Soph," Theo said.

"I have to rehearse for the pageant," Sophie pointed out. "Besides, Gug likes it."

And he did. Gug clapped with the rhythm and tried to sing along—*Tea, tea two. Tea, tea two*—and then reached for the cookie bag Sophie had opened, but Olivia swooped in and snatched it away, quickly replacing it with a bag of pretzel logs.

"No sugar, remember, Gug?"

Gug frowned and licked a pretzel log. He made a face. "Gug no like," he protested. "Gug want cook-a goo."

"Sorry, pal, but sugar makes you nuts," Olivia reminded.

"Yeah, it makes you crazy!" Sophie laughed, jumping on Gug and tickling him. Gug cackled and fell backward off of the carpet roll and onto the garage floor. A few of the dogs that had been sleeping on an old mattress in the corner hurried over and began licking Gug's face. He laughed hysterically. Then Sophie leapt on top of him and continued her tickle assault and thank goodness she did because just then Mrs. Bartlett entered.

"Hey, kids, who wants to go to the mall to get their picture taken with Santa?!" she said excitedly.

"Sure, Mom," Theo and Olivia both said quickly, terrified their mother would see Gug without his winter clothes on.

"Okay, Momma," Sophie giggled from behind the carpet roll where she and Gug couldn't be seen.

"Okay, Momma Bartlett," Gug laughed.

"My, his English is improving by leaps and bounds," their mother said as she left the garage.

Olivia and Theo looked at each other with great concern.

"I thought you locked the door!" Theo accused.

"I thought you did," Olivia protested.

Their mother walking in with Gug not in disguise was too close a call, they all agreed. So they promised each other to be more careful as no one else could know about Gug but the three of them.

And that's how it remained.

No one else would know.

Well, at least for the next forty-five minutes.

CHAPTER 20

A CRAZY TRIP TO THE MALL

DALTONS WAS THE fanciest department store in all of southern
New Hampshire, possibly even the whole state. Its entrance had twenty-
foot automatic doors and its outdoor Christmas lights could be seen all the
way from the top of McLean Pass, almost a half mile away. It was the
crown jewel of the Millbrook Falls Mall.

During the entire car ride to Daltons, the Bartletts sang Christmas carols. Mrs. Bartlett taught Gug "Silent Night" and "Little Drummer Boy" and
"Over the River and Through the Woods" which wasn't really a Christmas
song but it has the words *sleigh* and *snow* in it so they all sang it anyway.

Gug got some of the words but had trouble with others—but he
didn't care. It just felt so good to be with a *family*. His missed his own family
terribly, yet being with these strange but wonderful earthlings made his
homesickness a little bit easier to take.

Mrs. Bartlett had packed some carrot sticks and celery for the kids to
snack on and though they weren't as tasty as cook-a-goo's, Gug still liked
them a lot. In fact, he was growing very fond of Mr. and Mrs. Bartlett.

Mrs. Bartlett had made him something she called *pancakes* that morning and patted him on top of his hat as he left for school. He knew that was
a kind gesture because his own mother did that to him before he went out
to play *Zepkanab* with his brothers and sisters.

And Mr. Bartlett always smiled at Gug and hummed pleasantly to himself while he worked in his study. That was a habit Gug's own father had
when he would tinker with *Bork-knobs* in the family tool shed.

"Gug, I want you to experience all of the American Christmas tradi-
tions while you're staying with us," Mrs. Bartlett said enthusiastically as they

crossed the grand entrance into Daltons. "And no Christmas is complete until you get your photo taken with Santa Claus."

As they walked through the Sporting Goods Department, Gug was overwhelmed with the sights and sounds. Wonderful music played over speakers imbedded in the ceiling and blinking lights—like the ones on the tree at Tutu, Soapy and Liv-a's house—seemed to hang from every corner of every wall.

Gug softly *oooooo'd* and *aaaaaaah'd* as they made their way through the store. Theo and Olivia looked around, anxious—worried that someone would see that the boy under the hat and scarf and puffy jacket wasn't really a boy at all.

As they all moved through *Women's Clothing*, they passed a young boy wearing a red cap with a white pom-pom ball on top. Gug's eyes grew wide.

"Santa hat," Gug pointed as the boy went by.

"That's right, Gug," Olivia said. "Just like Santa's hat."

Gug reached into a bin and snagged a large size bra and wrapped it around his head.

"Look," Gug called out. "Santa hat."

Theo almost choked on his candy cane as Olivia quickly snatched off the bra and threw it into a shelf of sweaters.

"Just don't touch anything, okay, Gug? We can't draw attention to you. We have to protect you. Understand?"

Gug looked at her. He understood. Liv-a wanted him kept safe. He nodded. "Ok, Liv-a," he said.

The line to get your picture taken with Santa wasn't too long. While they waited, a pretty little girl waiting in line introduced herself to the Bartlett children.

"I'm Daisy," she said. "I'm four years old. I'm going to tell Santa I want a Unicorn Princess Doll and a Puppy Cuddles Play Set."

"That's great," Olivia said.

"Because I've been soooooooo good," Daisy continued, blinking her chocolate-brown eyes expressively as she talked. "I eat all the food on my plate—even the food I don't like—and I always turn the light off in the bathroom when I'm done because my Daddy doesn't own the 'lectric company and I help my Grandma Maime walk down the steps because she is sooooooo old. So I know Santa will bring me the toys I love!"

Theo and Olivia shared a concerned look. They didn't have the heart to tell Daisy that there might not be a Christmas this year because Santa's sleigh and all his presents—including her Princess Unicorn and Puppy Cuddles Play Set—were half buried in the snow in the woods behind their house!

"We really gotta fix this mess or there are gonna be a lot of disappointed kids in a few days," Theo said quietly to Olivia.

Olivia nodded in agreement.

Soon enough it was the Bartlett family's turn.

Theo and Olivia stood on either side of Santa so Mr. Bartlett could place Sophie on Santa's right knee and Gug on the left. Theo took a good look at Santa and was glad he didn't have to sit on this guy's lap. He was grumpy and looked mean and his beard smelled like pepperoni and sausage.

And the truth was, Artie Sneed was grumpy and mean, and if you asked him, he had darn good reason to be. He was nearing the end of a nine-hour shift during which all the children of Millbrook Falls had been plunked onto his knees, which were now killing him. Not to mention his back was tight as a drum thanks to the uncomfortable chair the mall had provided. And to top it off, he had only gotten fifteen minutes for lunch and the only thing he had time to eat was a greasy, cold slice of pepperoni and sausage pizza from the Food Court.

But Artie had no choice—he couldn't quit. He had to pay back Mr. Lipson for the five hundred dollar fine. So he just continued at a job that he hated with all his heart.

And when Gug turned to Artie, thinking he was Santa, Artie was in no mood to talk.

"Santa?" Gug asked. "Gug no mad. Gug knows accident. Santa good."

"Yeah, whatever, kid," Artie grumbled as the photographer got his camera ready.

"Santa no mean smash Gug," Gug said, trying to be friendly and make peace with the man in the red suit.

"Gug, this isn't the real Santa. He's just a helper," Olivia said, trying to get Gug to calm down.

"I got two kids on my lap here," Artie called out. "Can we take the picture already?"

"Got a problem with the camera," the photographer said as she fumbled with her equipment.

"Santa take Gug back up home?" Gug asked hopefully, pointing up to the ceiling with his finger. But his finger accidentally caught on Santa's beard.

"Get your finger outta my beard, kid!" Artie grumbled. But Gug's fingers were thick and they got tangled easily with the fake beard hair. He tried to pull his finger free but he yanked too hard and the beard snapped off Artie's face.

This scared the heck out of Gug who thought Santa's face had fallen off!

"Guuuuug!" the alien shrieked, shaking so much that his scarf slipped down, exposing his alien face to Artie (and luckily only to Artie as Gug's back was facing the crowded mall).

"Aaaaaah!" screamed Artie and he *leapt up*, sending Sophie and Gug tumbling over the side of his chair into a pile of fake snow and empty boxes wrapped up like Christmas presents as part of the display.

"Children!" Mrs. Bartlett cried as she made her way through the crowd, trying to get to Gug and Sophie.

Theo and Olivia hurried to Gug whose hat had now fallen off, exposing his bugle-shaped ears. With Theo and Olivia blocking Gug from one side, and the Christmas tree blocking him from the other, no one could see the young space creature.

No one but Artie Sneed that is.

"He's an alien! An alien!" Artie shouted at the top of his lungs as Theo and Olivia quickly covered him back up.

"I beg your pardon!" Mrs. Bartlett snapped as she broke through the crowd and hurried to a now disguised Gug's side. "He is a *Resident* Alien here legally from Iceland, thank you very much."

She gathered up her children and Gug and hurried off.

"But … but …" Artie stammered.

"You know, I work with children as a magician," Mr. Bartlett addressed Artie. "And you, sir, should not be working with children."

Mr. Bartlett turned and left.

"I agree with him," said Mr. Lipson who had hurried over from the Christmas Ornament Kiosk when he heard all the racket. "You're fired, Sneed. Turn in your beard and go home."

As the manager stormed off, Artie turned and glared at the Bartlett family walking away across the main mezzanine. He saw the alien that they were trying to pass off as a human boy. But he saw more than that. He saw *dollar signs!* He knew that alien would be able to help him pay off the five hundred dollar fine plus a heck of a lot more! Sneed had a plan!

Theo and Olivia both happened to look back over their shoulders at this exact moment.

They wished they hadn't ... because they could tell from the angry look on the now fired Santa's face that they had not seen the last of Artie Sneed.

CHAPTER 21
GREAT MINDS THINK ALIKE

"HEY, DID YOU hear all that ruckus? I think the Take Your Picture With Santa guy went crazy or something," Chester Flint said as he set a tray of food down at the Food Court table where his brother Jimmy jotted down notes on a piece of paper.

"I said did you hear the ruckus?" Chester repeated trying to get his brother's attention. Sometimes it seemed to Chester like he'd been trying to get his brother's attention his whole life and nothing ever seemed to work. And sometimes that would make him pretty sad.

But Jimmy just kept drawing on his paper. He used a small ruler and a protractor to make angels and then measure them; he'd fill out complicated math problems that had more letters than numbers. Then he'd find a mistake in his work, erase it and start all over again.

"Uh, I got you cheesy fries," Chester offered.

Jimmy just reached out without looking up from his paper, grabbed some fries and shoved them into his mouth.

"I was thinking, Jimmy, maybe this could be the wrong town—"

"No!" Jimmy interrupted like a madman. "This is the right town. My calculations are correct. Santa is somewhere in Millbrook Falls. But where? Because Santa crashing into a small town would kinda make the news, don't you think? But there's no Santa. Where's Santa?!" Jimmy shouted.

"Uh … the North Pole?" Chester offered humorously, trying to lighten the mood.

Jimmy just looked at his brother for a silent moment.

"Do you want to be a big buffoon your entire life, Chester?"

"Um … no?"

"Would you like to do something important for once? Something important like catch Santa Claus for all the world to see?"

"Uh, I guess. I mean, if that's what _you_ want to do."

Jimmy rubbed his face. The utter stupidity of his lummox brother never failed to amaze him.

"Yes, Chester. That's what I want to do. That's all I've ever wanted to do **since I was ten years old, you moron!** Now I'm thinking maybe this town isn't talking about Santa crashing here because they <u>don't know</u> he crashed here. Let's find out if there are any woods or state parks around here where he could've landed. No one would see him if there's a lot of tree coverage, right?" Jimmy theorized.

Chester just nodded with a mouth full of food.

"Then stop eating and let's go. He's somewhere in this stupid town and I'm going to find him!"

Jimmy got up and stormed off. Chester grabbed the cheese fries and hurried after. In fact he rushed so hard that he almost bumped into a family that was exiting the store—a family consisting of a mother, father, three children and one foreign exchange student from Iceland ... or Ghana ... depending on who you asked.

CHAPTER 22
SANTA PLAYS THE
CELEBRITY CARD

THE TRIAL OF Elvis and Santa had been going on for days and didn't seem to have an end in sight. The aliens kept shouting questions at the earthlings but Elvis and Santa couldn't understand them. No matter how many times Santa tried to explain who he was, it didn't help.

The two creatures that had caught them with the web shooter were frantically shouting at the judges and pointing at Elvis and Santa. And the little green guys who had chased them were seated, every day, in a penned-in area, shooting mean looks at the elf and the man in red.

And to make matters even worse, one of the space cops had been tinkering with a metallic device that had several switches, a large dial and a small satellite-thingy on top of it that he had turned and pointed right at the North Pole prisoners on several occasions. Elvis was convinced the device was meant to vaporize them and every time it was pointed at them he closed his eyes tight.

And on this particular day, the space cop jumped up excitedly as the metallic weapon began to make a buzzing sound. He ran to the judge and gave him the device.

The judge pointed the small satellite dish at Santa and Elvis and began turning the dial back and forth as a high frequency squeal filled the room.

"Oh man," Elvis said, worried. "This is it; they're gonna zap us! If this is the end, I want you to know that it's been an honor serving with you, sir."

"Oh, Elvis," Santa said reassuringly. "I don't think these creatures mean us harm. They are just confused and a little scared, that's all."

"How do you know?!" Elvis cried. "You can't tell for sure who's bad and who's nice!"

Santa raised an eyebrow at Elvis in a way that said, *Are you sure about that? Remember whom you're talking to.*

"Oh yeah," Elvis corrected himself, embarrassed. "I guess you can … but I'm still worried about these LITTLE GREEN SAVAGES!"

That last part—the part about "little green savages"—echoed loud and clear across the courtroom as if amplified by a microphone. Every alien gasped.

"What was that you called us, prisoner?" the Head Judge demanded. "Little green savages?"

"Holy smokes! He can understand us! And *I* can understand *him*!" Elvis shouted.

"Now that we've *finally* got our translator working, we are able to communicate in your rudimentary language," the Head Judge continued.

"Please excuse my friend," Santa stated. "We don't think you're savages. We think you are confused. You see, we are from Earth. And we are friendly—"

"They are NOT friendly," cried the alien with the full lips and almond eyes. "If you were friendly why did we find you on our ship! Why is one of my sons missing! They kidnapped him!"

"Uh … oh," Elvis whispered to Santa, putting together what was going on. "We are in big trouble."

"Kidnap? Why, I would never hurt a child! I have been bringing joy to children for hundreds of years!" Santa protested.

"Were you in their ship?" the Head Judge asked, pointing to Gug's parents.

"Yes," Santa answered.

"How did you get there?"

"I … I don't know," Santa stammered.

"And their son is now missing?" the judge continued.

"I have no reason to think these parents are lying. They are clearly worried for their child—"

"Then it is the ruling of this court that you are hereby found … GUILTY! Guilty of trespassing, guilty of kidnapping, guilty of—"

"—Um, Judge!" shouted an alien, in what appeared to be some kind of Court Officer's uniform, as he burst through the courtroom's door. "I think you need to see this. I've been trying to get information about the prisoners, see if they were wanted for crimes in any other galaxies, and I found _this_ in the intergalactic archives."

The Court Officer pressed a button on a small electronic pad and a hologram began to play. In front of the entire courtroom, the history of Santa and Christmas was told in crystal clear 3D. It explained the story of Christmas, how Santa travelled the entire world in one night, how his reindeer could fly, and most importantly, how he was loved by all the children of the world.

When the presentation was over, all the aliens slowly turned and looked at Santa in awe.

Santa just nodded. "Yeah," he smiled. "I'm kind of a big deal."

CHAPTER 23

AN UNEXPECTED GUEST
IN THE WOODS

OVER THE NEXT several days, Olivia, Theo, Sophie and Gug worked together to put Olivia's plan into action. There was a great deal that needed to be done and there was not a lot of time to do it as Christmas Eve was just four days away.

Olivia was in charge of getting the clear plastic sheet they'd place over the signal light that was going to be shone up into the night sky. She asked Mrs. Lavern, the art teacher, if she could have a few feet of cellophane for a project she was doing at home. Olivia didn't like to lie—certainly not to an adult—and *especially* not to a teacher—but she figured that she and the others were *kind of* doing a project. It wasn't exactly an *art* project, but it was a project to get Gug back home so Olivia rationalized that she wasn't really lying. Mrs. Lavern was in a rush to get to her lunch break after period four so she just said, "Sure thing, Ms. Bartlett. Take what's left on that roll over there by the paper cutter," as she was hurrying out the door. So the cellophane was taken care of. All that was left were the flashlights and the generator!

Sophie and Gug handled the flashlights. There were many of them stored all over the house in case of a power outage from a blizzard in the winter or a lightning storm in the summertime. They found two in the kitchen junk drawer, one in each of her parents' nightstands and a bunch of old ones scattered about in her father's workbench area in the garage. They even found a big one with a square light in the trunk of Mrs. Bartlett's car. Sophie also used some of the money she had saved from the tooth fairy and from birthdays to buy a few cheap plastic ones from the corner pharmacy that was just a block away from their house. She was certain they had more than enough. The plan was coming together. She just hoped Theo could handle the generator.

The generator was heavy and the night they all snuck out of the house to set up the signal, Theo had a really hard time dragging it through the snow, all the way from their backyard shed to where they had left the sleigh in the woods. He had barely gotten it up Miller's Hill—he pulled and Gug pushed from behind. For a little guy, Gug was pretty strong. By the time they got the generator to where the sleigh had landed, Theo and Gug were exhausted. Sophie and Olivia had already begun fastening all of the flashlights together with rope.

"There you are," Olivia said. "I was beginning to worry the generator got stuck in the snow."

"No, we got it," Theo said pushing the generator a few more inches and then collapsing onto his back into a pile of wrapping paper and ribbons that had fallen from Santa's sleigh when it crashed. Theo was breathing heavy—completely spent. Gug fell to the ground as well, catching his own breath.

"Gug ... need ... break," he panted.

Olivia looked at the huge generator with rusted wheels that barely turned and could only imagine how hard it was for her brother and Gug to get it so deep into the woods. She put her hand on Theo's shoulder.

"Hey," she said. "Good work. I know that thing's heavy as heck."

It felt strange for Olivia to give Theo a compliment—she couldn't remember the last time she did since it seemed they had been fighting or insulting each other forever. But they were in this thing together and it was just so much nicer when they were getting along.

"Do ... you ... have ... the ... picture?" Theo asked her in between gasps for air.

Olivia nodded and took a roll of cellophane paper from a brown cardboard box she had carried to the woods with Sophie. She unrolled it to reveal an outline of a picture made with a black marker. The picture looked like a coloring book page before it was colored in.

Gug looked at the picture and smiled.

"Is Gug!" he exclaimed.

"I did it all free hand," Sophie blushed. "I'm glad you like it."

"It's great," Theo said, amazed that a five year old could draw so well.

"Ok," Olivia said, determined. "Let me shed a little light on this situation."

Theo watched in awe as his sister opened all of the flashlights and removed the batteries. She then took an extension cord with one end cut off so that all the wires were exposed. She connected a single wire to each of the metal bottoms of the flashlights' light bulbs. When she was done, she propped up the bouquet of flashlights in the cardboard box and then plugged in the other end of the extension cord to the generator.

As she put her finger on the switch of the generator, Gug asked tentatively, "Liv-a? Will work?"

"Only one way to find out, pal," Olivia said. She flipped the switch on the generator and it sputtered to life. Then, slowly, the flashlight bulbs all began to glow and soon there was a bright light shining up high in the sky.

Theo couldn't help but be impressed by his sister.

"Man," Theo said kindly. "You've gotta be the smartest person I know."

Olivia blushed.

"Now for the picture," Sophie said. She took the cellophane drawing of Gug and carefully laid it over the flashlights, immediately projecting an image of Gug's face up high into the heavens. She then taped it down so it wouldn't blow away.

They all just stared at the sky's newest constellation for a moment.

"Wow," Olivia said softly. "We did it."

"Now all we have to do is hope Gug's family sees it. They bring Santa back and Gug gets to go home."

Sophie looked at Gug sadly. She wanted him to see his family, but she didn't want him to go home either.

"Won't someone in town see it?" Theo asked, surprised he hadn't thought of that question before.

"No, because of the same reason no none has found the sleigh yet. We're too deep in the woods," Olivia explained. "Plus, there are all the streetlights and car lights and Christmas lights back in town—it makes it harder to see light in the sky. That's why it always looks like there are more stars in the sky when you get away from a city."

"If you say so," Theo deferred. "I'll come back every day to add some gas to the generator. Dad's got two big gas cans full in the garage. But we need to get home, before anyone knows we're not in bed."

He quickly taped a note to the generator for Gug's family explaining that they have Gug and giving the Bartlett family's address. Theo ended the note with the following: *Please don't be offended, but I suggest you try to contact us in a way that you aren't seen by anyone. People on earth get a little freaked out by aliens. Even we were at first.* And in the envelope he included a picture of him, Olivia, Sophie and Gug. They all looked happy—this way Gug's parents would know right away that their son was okay.

As they ran back home, hurrying through the woods, they found the trip much easier without having to carry all the supplies but also because they all felt good that they were at least trying to make things better, even though they knew their plan was a million-to-one shot.

But that good feeling didn't last too long because when they turned the corner around Old Face Tree, they smashed right into Jimmy Flint. Jimmy fell backwards into Chester and they <u>both</u> fell backwards into the snow.

"Oh … sorry, mister," Theo said, extending a hand to help Jimmy up.

"It's *Airman*," Jimmy corrected as he stood, dusting snow off of himself. "Airman First Class James Flint."

"I'm Chester," Chester said with a smile. "Hi."

Jimmy eyed the kids suspiciously. They seemed nervous.

"What are you kids doing out in the woods in the middle of the night?" Jimmy asked.

"Ummm, stargazing," Olivia said. "We like stars."

"This late at night?" Jimmy pressed.

"Can't see 'em during the day," Sophie offered. It was a simple answer, but it made sense.

Gug looked at the Airman stripes sewn to Jimmy's uniform. They had a star in the middle and it captivated Gug.

"Oooooh, pretty," Gug said reaching for the star.

Flint slapped Gug's hand away. "Hands off the uniform, junior," he said, then turning to Theo, asked, "This kid talks funny. What's his deal?"

"He's from Iceland."

"So, listen," Jimmy tried to sound casual. "You kids see anything strange out over these woods the past few days ... like a small plane or aircraft—"

"—Or a sleigh," Chester interrupted.

Oooof! Jimmy slammed his hand into Chester's ample tummy as a signal to shut the heck up. But the kids heard him. They were looking for Santa's sleigh!

"A sleigh?" Olivia said, playing dumb. "Kids have sleighs in the woods all the time. They go down Miller's Hill."

"Not that kind of sleigh," Chester blurted. "The kind that Santa—"

Oooof! Another slam into Chester's stomach courtesy of his big brother.

"Well, it's late. I think you guys should head on home. But if you see anything out here—anything strange or weird or ... big and red ... you call the New England Division of NORAD and ask for Jimmy Flint. Got it?"

"Got it," all three kids said.

"Gug-a-boob," Gug said.

Jimmy looked at Gug for a moment.

"Strange language, that Icelandic," he commented. And then he and Chester were off. But as the children passed, Jimmy noticed something—a long piece of Christmas ribbon stuck to Theo's shoe.

"He's in these woods somewhere," Jimmy snarled to Chester. "I feel it in my bones."

CHAPTER 24
ALL WE NEED IS A
LITTLE BIT OF PUCK

IT WAS DECEMBER 21st and the Bartlett kids and Gug were very worried as they walked to school. There were only three more days until Christmas Eve, not to mention the fact that they found the United States Air Force in the woods looking for Santa's sleigh.

"Maybe he wanted to help Santa?" Sophie theorized. "The Air Force is good."

"The Air Force *is* good," Theo agreed. "But I just got a weird feeling from that Jimmy guy. I mean, if he was there to help Santa, why do it by sneaking around the woods in the middle of the night? No, I'm telling you, that guy's trouble."

"Speaking of trouble …" Olivia said, pointing.

Theo's eyes followed the direction of Olivia's finger to find world-class bully Winston Polenski angling across the street toward them with determined purpose. He looked much angrier than usual. In fact, he looked furious.

"Hey, Fartlett!" he shouted, drawing attention from all the other kids that were headed to school. "Where do you and your friend think you're going?"

By now a crowd had started to form. Felix wandered over from the corner where he had been showing off for 5th graders by juggling snowballs. And to make matters worse, Lisa had been walking across the Crooked Creek Bridge when Winston started shouting, so she and her friends had made their way over to see what all the commotion was about.

"You think you and your pal can just blow snot all over my mug and get away with it?" Winston barked.

"It wasn't snot," Theo said, scared.

"Oh, yeah?" Winston asked. "Then what was it, smart guy?"

"Um ... *mucus?*"

The crowd of kids laughed. But not Theo ... and definitely not Winston.

"You think you're funny?" Winston said stepping to Theo.

Olivia instinctively moved closer to her brother.

Winston snickered. "You need your little sister to protect you?"

The crowd chuckled again, this time at Theo's expense.

"Leave my brother alone, Winston!" Sophie shouted.

"Winston?" Gug said, suddenly remembering. "Winston's a dillweed!"

Oooooooooooooo, the school kids all crowed. They had never seen anyone brave or crazy enough to call Winston a name before.

Winston turned red. He was livid. "What was that?" the bully fumed.

"Winston's a dillweed! Winston's a dillweed! Winston's a dillweed!" Gug sang to the amusement of the spectators.

"Ok, then," he said through gritted teeth. "The principal says if I beat up any more nerds this semester I'll get expelled."

"Well ... Principal Kugler is a very smart man ..." Theo stammered.

"*But* ..." Winston continued, "he didn't say anything about me pounding them into the ice during a friendly little game of hockey. So ... your team vs. mine—after school—or come January, when a new semester starts, it'll be open season on you and your weird little friend here. Understood?"

"Well, there's a lot of kids on the team," Theo sputtered. "And some of them might not be able to make it on such short notice—"

"—You're team captain. If you call a game, they have to show. Those are the rules. So I'll see you at 3:30 at the lake. You got that, Fartlett?"

Theo swallowed hard. He was dead either way. His team stunk and hadn't won a game in over a year while Winston's team was undefeated—their roster was made up of the biggest and meanest kids in town and their record stood at 11-0. Theo knew if he got on the ice he would be demolished by Winston and his goon squad. But he also knew if he didn't accept the challenge, he would spend the entire second semester being tormented by the same kids. He figured it was best to just take his medicine and get it over with.

"Yeah, I got it," Theo mumbled.

"Got it, Dillweed," Gug called out.

Winston glared at Gug. "I wanna see you out on the ice too, freak-a-zoid," Winston growled before storming off. The crowd slowly dispersed. A few kids just shook their heads at Theo, sorry for what was about to happen to him. Others were secretly looking forward to watching a good brain beating on Lake Clearwater.

That afternoon the lake was packed. Every kid in town seemed to come out to see the massacre. Olivia and Sophie sat in the bleachers. Olivia hoped for a good outcome but just in case she had stopped by the nurse's office after school and picked up a small first aid kit.

Lisa and her friends were there as well. Theo watched her as he warmed up on the ice. The last thing he wanted was to be humiliated in front of Lisa Connelly but it seemed like that was his destiny. Theo had Gug playing goalie because between the goalie mask, pads, gloves and jersey there was no way anyone could tell that there was an alien on the ice. Theo had asked their regular goalie, Danny Krump, if he could let the foreign exchange student play in his place. Normally Danny would never want to miss a game but he had heard (just like everyone else in the school) that Winston and his crew were planning on creaming Theo's team into a million tiny pieces—so Danny Krump happily sat this game out.

Once the game started it was everything Theo had feared and more. Winston plowed him into the ice, flipped him over snow banks and completely out of the rink, and body-checked him so hard that Theo was almost knocked from his skates. And when he wasn't beating up on Theo he was taking it out on Felix who was such a slow skater he couldn't avoid a single collision.

Winston's team was so intent on physically punishing their opponent that they didn't bother to take a single shot on goal. They couldn't have cared less about scoring—they knew by the end of the game they'd shoot a puck or two into the net to keep their undefeated streak alive, but for now all they cared about was crushing the other team as much as possible.

Gug watched all of this from the goal. He didn't completely under-stand all of the rules of the game but Theo had explained it was Gug's job to stop the puck from going into his net while Theo's job was to put the puck into the <u>other</u> net. But what Gug didn't understand was why the one human the other kids called Winston (or *Dillweed*) was pushing everyone over on the ice in such a violent manner. It seemed to Gug that Winston was trying to intentionally hurt Theo and it made him angry.

So when the puck finally slid to Gug late in the third period he decided to do something about it. Instead of just passing the puck to one of his teammates—as any normal goaltender would—he began skating up the ice with it! When an opponent came at Gug he wiggled his rubbery body right around the guy, leaving his opposition grasping at air. He contorted his pli-able alien frame between players, under their sticks and around their legs! He was incredible! Everyone on Winston's team was trying to get Gug and they couldn't even come close!

This went on for several minutes with Winston screaming at his play-ers to "just get the little weirdo already!" But they simply couldn't. He was too elusive. Theo, Felix and the rest of their teammates simply stopped skating after a while and watched Gug in stunned silence.

"Go, Gug!" Sophie shouted. Olivia whooped and clapped. Soon everyone was cheering for Gug. Gug turned and waved at everyone. He was really enjoying himself. In fact he was enjoying himself so much that he didn't notice Winston bearing down on him with a full head of steam!

But Theo did.

"Gug!" he warned.

Gug spun to find Winston barreling at him at full speed—just inches away from flattening Gug like a pancake.

Gug instantly reacted. In a split second he threw his goalie stick up and over Winston's head then dropped on his side and **<u>slid</u>** under the bully, between his legs, and popped up on the other side. Winston, still moving across the ice at great speed, turned his head just in time to see Gug <u>*catch*</u> his stick and slap the puck past Winston's goalie just as the buzzer sounded to end the game!

Theo's team won 1-0!

Winston was so amazed at the most incredible hockey move he'd ever seen that he forgot he was still streaking across the ice heading right toward a snow bank! He smashed into it, flipped into the air and landed in it head first. Just his legs stuck out, waving around futilely.

Everyone surrounded Gug, patted him on the back and congratulated him on his amazing goal.

"Man," Felix said amazed. "Where'd he learn to play like that?"

"Iceland, I guess," Theo answered, astounded.

"Great game, Theo," Lisa said with a smile as she walked by.

"Lisa?" Gug squealed. "Tutu *loves* Lisa!"

Theo's mouth fell open. Felix stifled a laugh. Lisa and her friends just giggled and continued across the frozen lake.

"Well, Tutu," Felix said putting his arm around his buddy. "At least now she knows how you feel."

CHAPTER 25
A JUICY STORY

NEW HAMPSHIRE BELL had cut off Artie Sneed's phone service because he hadn't paid his bill in over four months and since he hadn't held a steady job in years he couldn't afford a cell phone. So even though he didn't want to make a phone call of such a sensitive nature from one of the few remaining public phone booths in Millbrook Falls, he didn't have much of a choice. But at least this pay phone was behind Millbrook Auto Body amongst the weeds. No one really walked back there so it was pretty private.

He dug around in the pocket of his dirty jeans and pulled out three nickels and one dime. He fed them into the phone and dialed a number he had scrawled onto a scrap of paper. After a few rings, an uninspired voice answered: "Marty Scratcher, *National Tattler.*"

"Yes, um, hello, Mr. Scratcher. I'm a big fan of your writing. I particularly enjoyed the piece on the wolfman boy that was born in Georgia …"

"What the heck's a wolfman boy?" Mr. Scratcher bellowed. "That makes no sense. Either you're a wolf<u>man</u> or a wolf<u>boy</u> and I covered the story of a wolf<u>boy</u>."

"My mistake. My mistake," Artie said trying to get back on Mr. Scratcher's good side. "Let me get to the point, sir. I'm calling because I heard you pay good money for amazing stories for your newspaper and I've got an amazing story for you."

"Oh yeah," the reporter said unimpressed. "And what's that?"

Artie looked around to make sure no one was listening. There was no one near.

"There is …" Artie paused for dramatic effect. "A real, live *alien* living in Millbrook Falls, New Hampshire."

"Really? Take a number and get in line," Scratcher guffawed.

"Maybe you didn't hear me correctly," Artie said, perturbed. "But there is an actual space alien running around this town! I saw him with my own eyes!"

"Oh yeah, where was he?" Marty asked.

"He was sitting on my lap," Artie answered.

"An alien was sitting on your lap?" Scratcher echoed in disbelief.

"Well, yeah. I was dressed in my Santa suit at the time—"

"Okay, nutball, I'll tell you the same thing I tell every lunatic who calls here screaming about aliens and goblins and little purple men—"

"—He's *green*," Artie said indignantly.

"Fine. Little *green* men. Whatever. The standing policy of *The National Tattler* is that <u>if you bring us the creature</u> we will pay one million dollars. Bring us the proof, you get the dough. We don't take witness statements, no photographs, no home movies. You bring that little gremlin in here and then you're rich. That simple. Clear enough for ya?"

"Yes, you got it, Mr. Scratcher. I'll get him for you. I'll bring him right to your desk," Artie promised.

"Ok. You go do that, Mr. Crazy," the reporter said before hanging up.

Artie stood there in the phone booth—a small, evil smile crossing his face. He had his marching orders. All he had to do was catch that little alien from the mall and he was a millionaire!

CHAPTER 26
HOME ALONE

AFTER THE HOCKEY game, Theo was certain that Winston was going to thump him into a fine powder, but since it was the end of first semester and the beginning of Christmas vacation, he knew he'd be able to avoid the bully for at least the next two weeks.

And the truth was, he had more important things to worry about. First and foremost was the fact that for the past three days there had been no response to the Gug Signal they'd shone up into the sky. Every morning, right before dawn, Theo would wake up and sneak out of the house and into the woods to turn off the generator. That was Olivia's idea—she said there was no use in having the generator run during the day since no one would be able to see the signal in the daylight.

Then, when the sun was about to set, Theo would hustle back out to the sleigh, put more gas in the generator, turn it back on and send the signal back up into the heavens. Before he left the woods each night, he said a little prayer: "Please let someone see this," he'd say softly before racing home.

But by Christmas Eve his prayers, and the prayers of the young Bartlett girls, had yet to be answered. After dinner that night, they all went upstairs to Theo's room with Gug to get ready for the school's Christmas Pageant Talent Show. Normally they'd be excited for the pageant—Theo and Felix were going to get to work the lights and the curtain, Olivia was going to play the National Anthem on her clarinet with the school band and Sophie was doing a ventriloquist routine with Opie. But instead of being excited, they were sad. They knew that the next morning children all over the world would wake up, run to their Christmas trees ... and find nothing.

And Gug knew that the chances of ever being reunited with his family were getting smaller and smaller by the day.

"Gug want see family," he said sadly as Olivia packed up her clarinet.

"I know you do," Theo said sitting next to Gug on the window seat. "Maybe they'll come tonight."

"But if they don't come tonight, when Santa <u>has</u> to be here to deliver presents, then when <u>*will*</u> they come?" Sophie asked, concerned.

Gug looked up at Olivia with sad eyes.

"Liv-a?" he said. "You find Gug family?"

Olivia had to fight back her tears. She knelt before her friend and put her hands on his shoulders, looking into his eyes.

"We tried, Gug. And we'll keep trying," she said. She didn't want to say what she said next as she always wanted to hold out hope that things would work out, but she felt Gug was feeling very alone and wanted to make him feel better. "But if things don't turn out the way we want," she continued, "You'll always have us. Me, Soapy, Tutu and Mom and Dad. You can always be part of our family if you want. Okay?"

But Gug just looked at her. He said nothing.

"Ok, kids!" Mr. Bartlett shouted from downstairs. "The Christmas Pageant Express is ready to roll! All aboard!"

Gug stood up, pulled on a Millbrook Falls Hockey T-Shirt and began wrapping his scarf around his face.

"No, Gug, you need to stay here tonight," Theo said kindly.

"Gug no come?" the alien asked, confused.

"It's just that I'll be backstage working the lights, Olivia will be with the band, Sophie will be in the cafeteria waiting with the other acts to go on—you'd be with just Mom and Dad and it's not safe if one of us isn't with you at all times. It's for your own good."

Gug understood. But it didn't make him happy that he couldn't be with his earth family when he was feeling his lowest.

The kids all said goodbye to Gug and went downstairs. Olivia told a small fib that Gug wasn't really feeling that well and wasn't going with them.

The Bartlett's' parental instincts instantly kicked in.

"Do you want me to make you some chicken soup, Gug, sweetheart?" she called up the stairs.

"No thank-a-goo," he called back sadly.

"Oh, he sounds terrible," Mr. Bartlett said. "Maybe if I do some quick magic tricks for him it'll lift his spirits—"

"No," Olivia cut off her father and blocked him from going upstairs. "He said he was just feeling run down and tired and wanted to rest. You have to understand, in Iceland they're used to sleeping twelve hours a day."

"Really?" Mrs. Bartlett asked.

"Yeah—it's a different culture—and he's only been getting eight hours here. So he needs to catch up."

"Okay," Mrs. Bartlett called up the stairs. "But if you need anything, Gug, you call my cell phone, okay?"

"O.K.," Gug answered.

As the family exited the house, Theo whispered to his sister, "Man, for someone who doesn't like to lie you're amazing at it!"

Gug laid on Theo's bed, listening to the Bartlett's' car door slam. His eyes welled up with tears.

"Family!" he shouted and he ran as fast as he could out of the room, across the hall and down the stairs to the front door. He opened it to see the Bartlett car already backing out of the driveway. He raced back upstairs and ran to the window seat in Theo's room. He flung open the window just in time to see the car driving away.

"Family!" Gug cried out. "Family!"

But they did not hear him and Gug felt in his heart that once again he had lost his family.

So he ran out of the front door, over the lawn and down the street, mumbling "Family, family" over and over to himself.

He wore nothing but the Millbrook Falls Hockey t-shirt. Anyone could have seen him.

CHAPTER 27
GUG IS NO DUMMY

BY THE TIME the Bartletts got to the school it was jam-packed. It seemed all of Millbrook Falls had come out for the show. The parents of all the kids who were performing were there, not to mention some grand-parents. And all the kids who <u>weren't</u> performing were there to see their friends. Not to mention teachers, their guests, the mayor, the entire Millbrook Falls Town Council and way in the back of the auditorium, hid-den behind a pillar, was Artie Sneed—on the lookout for a group of kids and their little green friend.

The show went off without a hitch. Olivia and the rest of the school band played a lovely *Star Spangled Banner*. Theo and Felix did a great job on the lights and Lisa and her pals sang *Santa Baby* to a rousing ovation. Theo made sure to compliment Lisa when she came backstage after her song was through.

"Thanks, Theo," she said. "You did a great job on the lights." And then she and her pals ran off to get changed out of their costumes while Sophie entered the back stage area with Opie as they were the closing act of the night.

"First of all, I helped with the lights," Felix said. "And second of all, call me crazy, but I think Lisa might actually be starting to like you, butt-brain."

Theo couldn't believe it. *Lisa Connelly? Likes me? Could it be possible?*

His mind was swimming with romantic thoughts when the doors that led to the backstage area *flew open* and Gug, *in no disguise at all*, ran in!!!

"Soapy!" he cried out spotting, literally, his best friend on earth.

"Gug!" she shouted back.

"Oh no!" Theo shouted.

Felix just stood there in complete shock with his mouth hanging open—he couldn't believe what he was seeing.

Theo and Sophie ran to Gug.

What are you doing out of the house?! Where is your disguise?! What are you doing here?!

Their questions were fast and furious but Gug just kept saying, "*Family.* Gug no want alone. *Family.*"

Sophie and Theo grabbed Gug's hands. "We gotta get you outta here!" Theo said but before they could take a step back toward the exit, Principal Kugler hurried backstage.

Theo and Sophie and Gug all froze.

"There you are, Ms. Bartlett," he said, face buried in a clipboard holding a list of the show's acts. "You and your dummy are on." He pointed at Gug when he said *dummy.*

"No dummy. *Gug,*" Gug corrected.

Principal Kugler's eyes grew wide.

This is it, Theo thought. *We're busted.*

"Hey, you're pretty good at that," the principal smiled. "I just love ventriloquist acts. Now, let's go, missy. Get on out there."

He hustled Sophie and Gug out onto the stage. Sophie quickly put her hand up the back of Gug's shirt and whispered into Gug's ear. "You've seen me practice with Opie. Just do what he did and no one will know you're real. Got it?"

"Got it, Soapy," Gug whispered back.

Meanwhile, Felix, white as a ghost, looked to Theo. "Do you wanna tell me what the heck *THAT* was?!" he exclaimed.

"What do you think it was?" Theo asked cautiously.

"I think it was an alien!!"

"Well, you're right. I'll explain later. But for now, keep it to yourself."

"Ok," Felix said. "But if he melts my brain with a space ray you're disinvited to my birthday party."

Theo was no longer listening to Felix. He was too busy watching Sophie getting ready on a stool on stage with Gug on her lap. Principal Kugler gave Felix the signal to raise the curtain.

"Well, here goes nothing," Felix said as he began pulling the rope that lifted the curtain to reveal Sophie and Gug to the entire audience.

When Olivia saw Gug she dropped her clarinet.

When Artie Sneed saw Gug he gasped so hard he began choking on a piece of a Milky Way Bar that he was eating. He stumbled out of the back doors, pounding on his chest with his fist.

When Mr. and Mrs. Bartlett saw Gug, they asked each other, "When did Sophie get a new dummy?"

Sophie was nervous. She wasn't sure if she was going to fool anyone but she decided to give it her best shot. So she began her act. The first part was a comedy routine and luckily Gug had heard her rehearsing enough with Opie that he knew what to say.

"Hey, Gug?" she asked. "How do you like school?"

"Closed," Gug deadpanned in his strange alien voice that everyone thought was actually coming from Sophie.

The crowd roared with laughter.

"Why did the kid take a ladder to class?"

"Because he went to *high school*."

The crowd laughed even louder.

Mrs. Bartlett beamed with pride. "I can't believe how good she got at this," she said.

"Chip off the old block," Mr. Bartlett puffed. "A natural entertainer, just like her Dad."

Sophie and Gug did a few more jokes and ended with an oldie but a goodie.

"Why was the math book so sad?" Sophie proffered.

"Because it had so many problems," Gug responded.

By this third joke the crowd was *loving* Gug and Sophie. And even though Gug didn't really get the jokes, the laughter made him feel all warm and tingly inside—he loved seeing the earthlings smile and cheer. He liked making them happy.

"And now, we would like to do a dance number to one of the classics," Sophie announced. She turned and nodded to Theo who was still stunned that Gug was out in front of the whole town with no disguise and not only could no one tell, but they were applauding him! It may have been his dazed and confused state that caused Theo to not pay attention when he put the CD in the sound system and pressed play, because it wasn't until the first few beats of *I Feel Good* by James Brown blared over the speakers that Theo realized he had put in the wrong music!

Sophie looked at Gug who said "This no *Tea, Tea Two.*"

"I know," Sophie whispered, "just go with it."

So they both began to dance to the music. Sophie kept her hand up the back of Gug's shirt so it seemed like she was controlling him, but the truth was, the backbeat and the horns and the funky rhythm of James Brown is what <u>really</u> had control of Gug.

Before Sophie knew it, Gug was spinning and sliding and doing splits. Sophie could barely keep up, but somehow she did, throwing in her own slick moves as well.

The audience went wild! They stood up and whooped and hollered. Even Olivia and Theo forgot for a second that Gug could be discovered at any time and instead lost themselves in the fun of the moment.

At the end of the song, Gug did something that was not only amazing, but that also turned out to be his undoing. He grabbed the microphone and began singing and he danced James Brown-style across the stage with Sophie. *Gug feel good—him know that he would!* But right before the music ended he threw the microphone up in the air, slid under Sophie's legs and caught it before laying still, pretending to be nothing but a dummy! The crowd went nuts as it appeared to the entire audience that Sophie had pushed Gug through her legs in an amazing feat of showmanship.

Well, actually, not the <u>entire</u> audience. Because when Winston, who was seated in the middle of the fourth row, saw that move he instantly recognized it as the same move Gug pulled in the hockey game when he slid between *Winston's* legs.

"That's no dummy," Winston said softly to himself in a moment of realization. "That's the <u>goalie</u>!"

He knew something was up with that *thing* that everyone thought was a puppet and he was determined to find out what it was. He pushed his way through the standing ovation and out the back door, bumping into Artie Sneed who was making his way back in, pretty exhausted from spending the past five minutes coughing a Milky Way chunk out of his throat.

Artie got in just in time to see Sophie carrying Gug off stage like he was a doll. But Artie knew better.

"You might have everyone else fooled, kid," he scowled. "But you ain't foolin' me."

CHAPTER 28

A NEW PARTNERSHIP IS FORMED

"SO YOU'VE BEEN dragging an alien around all this time and I'm just finding out about it now!" Felix shouted at Theo.

"Shhhhh," Olivia hissed. "Our parents will hear you! The den is right below Theo's room."

"I'm just saying, we're supposed to be friends. I mean, this is *amazing*. You should've told me," Felix said, as he leaned in close to Gug, studying his face.

"Hi, Fuffa," Gug said.

"Felix," Felix corrected.

"Don't even bother," Theo said. "He calls me Tutu."

"Um … I wouldn't get too close to those if I were you," Olivia warned as Felix peered into Gug's huge bell-shaped ear-horn.

"Helloooooo down there," he called loudly into an ear.

"Gaaaaa," Gug bellowed, blowing his alien gunk all over Felix.

"Uggg! What is this stuff?!" Felix yowled, wiping the goop from his face with his shirt.

"I warned you," Olivia said. "How'd you like it if someone shouted into your oversized, sensitive ears?"

"Sorry, Fuffa," Gug said sheepishly. "Accident."

"So this is it?" Felix asked, his face now pretty clean. "This is the year Christmas ends … forever?"

"We've done everything we can think of," Theo said dejected.

And as the Bartlett kids explained to Felix all about the signal in the woods and how there had been no response to it, they were unaware that in the tree right outside Theo's window, Artie Sneed was lying on his belly on a branch twenty feet off the ground, getting a good look at all of them … *especially Gug.*

"I am going to be a wealthy man," he squealed, wriggling forward, trying to get a closer look. But when he did, his weight shifted and the tree branch snapped a bit. This made two of the Bartlett's' bigger dogs—Beauregard and Blackjack—lift their heads up from Theo's floor where they were sleeping. Ears perked, they instinctively turned to the window and saw Artie hiding in the darkness, looking right back at them. Beauregard and Blackjack were both Boxers—a lovely breed of dog that is quite sweet and gentle … unless someone messes with their family.

Ruhr Ruhr Ruhr Ruhr Ruhr, the dogs barked as they leapt at the window furiously, incredibly protective of the Bartlett children. Artie flinched, lost his balance and began to slip from the branch. He reached out to grab something—*anything*—to stop him from falling but only got a handful of air. He plummeted toward the ground expecting a hard landing, but instead something pretty soft broke his fall.

"Oooof!" Winston called out as Artie landed right on top of him. The two of them rolled around on the ground for a second, untangling their limbs.

"What the heck, man?" Winston spat. "You could've killed me!"

"Well," Artie bumbled as he brushed himself off. "What are you doin' skulking around in the bushes out here at night, kid?"

"Name's Winston, not *kid*. And you're one to talk. What are you doin' jumpin' on people from trees, ya whacko?"

"I didn't jump. I fell. And I was up there bird watching."

"At nine-thirty at night?" Winston said dubiously.

"Ever hear of owls?" Artie shot back.

"Ever hear of *you're a liar*?" Winston responded. "You were peeping into the house."

"Yeah, like you're one to talk," Artie countered, pointing to the first floor window that Winston was clearly looking into when Artie fell on him. "Now why don't you tell me what you're lookin' for."

Winston sized Artie up. "Why don't *you* tell *me*?" he asked.

Now Artie sized *Winston* up. Neither one of these guys trusted each other.

"Tell ya what. We say it on three. One ... two ... *three*."

And that's when Artie and Winston both shouted out *Little Green Guy*!

There was a moment of silence and then they smiled deviously at each other. They both knew that they had each found the partner they needed to catch their prey.

CHAPTER 29

UP IN THE SKY—IT'S A BIRD! IT'S A PLANE! IT'S ... SOME KID'S DRAWING OF AN ALIEN!

OOOOOOH!

Aaaaaaah!

The alien children cooed with wonder and amazement as they sat at Santa's feet toward the rear of the flight deck, watching him use his incredible magic to conjure toys out of practically anything Gug's brothers and sisters gave him.

A piece of paper instantly became a string of paper dolls. A ball of yarn became a marionette. And a bowl of orange mush with black specs in it—a "delicacy" that seemed to be all these aliens ate—became a superball that bounced all over the place. The little aliens chased the mush ball and Santa couldn't help but chuckle—children were the same no matter their age or country or even planet—they all loved to play.

Elvis wasn't chuckling however. After the intergalactic court realized who he and Santa were—and the theory of Santa's sleigh crashing into Gug's Starhopper was painstakingly fleshed out—they were set free and released into the custody of Gug's parents, whose names Elvis learned were Matto (the mother) and Donk (the dad). They had been flying their ship through space for days, trying to remember where they had been when they'd used the tractor beam to bring the children in from their Starhoppers. Neither parent seemed to have a good memory and Elvis was losing his patience.

"It's Christmas Eve!" he stressed to Matto and Donk. "We need to get Santa back to his sleigh within the next few hours!"

"Don't pressure me!" Donk shouted back. "I know your holiday is important to you but our son is important to us as well! We're doing the best we can!"

At the mention of Gug, Matto broke into hysterics for what seemed like the millionth time. "Oh, my poor baby!" she cried. "My poor baby boy, trapped on that savage planet!"

"Savage?" Elvis protested. "We're _nice_! You're the ones that tied us up and accused us of kidnapping!"

"Oh, he might catch some fearful disease down there!" she sobbed.

Annoyed, Elvis walked away, turning off the intergalactic translator as he left.

"Gaggle-ghibli-guff guff!" Matto rambled on, this time in her native tongue.

The elf slumped down in a chair next to Santa.

"I might have to listen to her," Elvis grumbled, "but I don't have to understand it."

"Be sympathetic and patient with her," Santa explained. "She's worried for her child. Try to imagine how she feels."

Elvis looked at Santa like he was nuts.

"How she feels?!" Elvis exploded. "What about how _I_ feel?! I've been working my elf tail off all year long, getting ready for _tonight_, and now we're gonna miss Christmas! Do you know how hard it will be to bounce back from something like this? The credibility issues we're going to have?! And you're just sitting here making toys like everything is going to be ok?"

"That's because everything will be okay," Santa said calmly.

"And how in Jack Frost's name do you know that?!" Elvis asked.

"Because I'm Santa," the big man said with a reassuring smile and a wink.

"Globbity Gazooooo!" Donk shouted loudly, jumping up and down excitedly. "Globbity Gazooooo!"

"We can't understand you, you crazy alien!" Elvis called out.

Donk flipped the translator back on. "Out there! Look! It's my son!"

Santa and Elvis rushed to the main control panel of the flight deck where Matto and Donk were pointing and grinning wildly out into space, which could be seen through a massive glass wall that was kind of like a car's windshield except a heck of a lot bigger.

Santa and Elvis looked out into the heavens and saw what was getting the alien mother and father so animated. There was a huge projection of a young alien's face far off in the distance. It was clearly coming from earth.

"It's a signal!" Matto shouted. "It's a signal from our baby!"

"It's not too much farther," Donk said, reading various gauges on the instrument panel. "We should be there soon."

And as the alien parents and children celebrated, Santa looked to his elf protégé.

"I told you everything would be ok," Santa gleamed.

"Nobody likes a know-it-all," Elvis snapped back.

Santa chuckled. He liked his elves spicy.

CHAPTER 30
ONE ZAMBONI,
PLEASE–HOLD THE ICE.

"THEO, SWEETIE," MRS. Bartlett called up the stairs to her son's room. "One of your friends stopped by to wish you a Merry Christmas."

"Friend?" Felix asked curiously. "I'm the only friend you have. And I'm already here."

The kids and Gug all hurried down the stairs, shocked to see who was waiting for them in the doorway with a fake smile plastered on his face.

"Merry Christmas, pal," Winston grinned.

Theo didn't know how to react, but the very idea that the school's #1 bully—his mortal enemy—was in his own house was absolutely bone chilling.

"Your father and I are running to the store to pick up some last minute items for Christmas dinner tomorrow," Mrs. Bartlett said as she bundled up.

Mr. Bartlett appeared from the living room, pulling on his coat.

"Felix, we'll take you home as soon as we get back. And Theo, your buddy can stay for a little while, but I want you guys in your jammy jams and in bed by 10:30 or Santa won't come tonight," Mr. Bartlett warned with a smile as he and his wife hurried out, closing the door behind them.

Theo had three horrible thoughts in quick succession:

1)   His dad didn't know it, but no matter how early they went to bed, Santa wasn't coming.

2)   Did his father just say *jammy jams* in front of
     Winston?!

3)   Winston was alone with them in their house!

Winston looked at the kids, loving the fact that they all seemed to be pretty freaked out by his presence. "I'll be quick," he said smugly, "since you don't want to be late getting into your *jammy jams*. I think you cheated the other day at the lake. This exchange student here, he must be some kind of professional hockey player where he comes from."

"I really don't think they have hockey where he comes from," Felix said, drawing a sharp elbow to the ribs from Olivia.

"Either you meet me at the lake in 10 minutes for a one-on-one skills competition or I drag you outside and beat you up on your own front lawn. Your choice."

"There are five of us, Winston," Olivia reminded. "Do you really believe you can take us *all* on?"

"Without breaking a sweat," Winston responded without hesitation. His confidence was unnerving.

"Um … I don't think my parents would like me going to the lake so late at night," Theo stammered.

"Oh, little chicken Bartlett, stinks like a Fartlett," Winston sang. Gug's blood boiled.

"Tutu no stink like fartlett," he defended. "*Winston* stink like fartlett."

"There ya go again, Fartlett, letting someone fight your battles for you," Winston taunted.

"No," Theo said, standing up straight and looking Winston right in the eyes. "I'm tired of you, Winston. The whole school is. I'll get my hockey gear and see you in ten minutes."

Winston smiled and left.

"He's gonna grind you into the ice, ya know," Felix said as soon as the front door closed.

"Probably," Theo said. "But if we can take care of an alien, hide him from our teachers, figure out where a space accident happened and shine a signal up into the galaxy, then we sure as heck can stand up to Winston Polenski."

"Heck yeah we can," Sophie shouted.

"Way to go," Olivia chimed in.

"Winston's a dillweed," Gug added for good measure.

The kids got their winter coats on, Theo grabbed his skates and his stick and they made their way to Clearwater Lake. They hustled because they had no idea when Mr. and Mrs. Bartlett would return home and if they were caught out of the house they would get in serious trouble. Also, Felix's parents told him he could stay late at Theo's but he had to be home by eleven o'clock. So they had no time to waste.

When they arrived at the lake it was pitch black out. The moon cast a bit of light on the frozen water so the kids could see where they were going as they shuffled across the ice. Theo's skates hung over his shoulder, their laces tied in a knot—his hockey stick that he had gotten from his Aunt Jo-Ann the prior Christmas, was held in his right hand.

They all looked around. No one was there.

"I can't believe it," Olivia said, amazed. "Winston chickened out. He didn't show."

"It's a Christmas Miracle," Sophie squealed happily.

"What time is it?" Theo asked.

"A minute after 10," Felix checked on his watch.

"Good enough for me," Theo concluded. "I was here. He wasn't. End of feud. I win."

But as they all turned to go they heard, "Leaving so soon, Fartlett?"

Their blood ran cold. They turned back to look into the darkness but no one was there.

Then they heard a man's voice yell *"Now!"* and all the overhead lights around the rink burst on at once. It was blinding for a moment but all of their eyes adjusted just in time to see Winston barreling at them holding three hockey sticks that were taped together.

While he charged them, the man who must have yelled *Now* leapt from behind the home team bench and threw a net over Gug! None of the Bartlett kids could have known this, but they had actually met this man once before—he had been wearing a Santa suit at the time and they were busy getting their picture taken with him at the mall!

Gug cried out and struggled as Artie Sneed grabbed him up and hurried off the lake to his wreck of an Oldsmobile.

"Gug!" Sophie cried. The kids tried to hurry after, but Winston had reached them at full speed, his huge, makeshift hockey stick barrier held in front of him. He crashed into the Bartletts and Felix, causing all of them to fall over like bowling pins.

"Have a nice fall, losers!" he cackled and then raced to the car as well.

"We're going to be rich!" Theo heard Artie scream as the car peeled off.

"They have Gug!" Olivia shouted as they all staggered to their feet.

"We'll never catch them!" Felix cried.

"Like heck we won't!" Theo yelled pointing to the Town of Millbrook Falls' Zamboni parked in the corner of the lake. "Get in!"

They moved as fast as they could to the giant vehicle, slip-sliding on the ice in their sneakers. As they climbed on, Olivia yelled, "Keys are in the ignition! But none of us know how to drive!"

"Felix does!" Theo shouted.

"I do?"

"Yeah, you drove at your uncle's farm," Theo reminded him.

"A tractor. Once. And I was sitting on his lap!"

"It's the same thing, except instead of driving across a field, you'll be driving across ice!" Theo reassured.

"Actually," Olivia said, "you'll be driving across Town Square because ... LOOK!"

Olivia had spotted the car, screeching around a corner about one hundred yards away.

"C'mon, Felix. We can catch them! They've got, Gug! We gotta go now!" Theo pleaded.

Felix thought about it for no more than a second. "No one steals my best friend's alien!" he declared and he started up the engine.

He popped the Zamboni into DRIVE and hit the accelerator. Unfortunately, Zambonis are designed to smooth out a hockey rink's ice so they don't move as fast as a car. But fortunately, Olivia was right about the shortcut across Town Square—at the angle they were moving, if Felix could just keep a decent speed going, they'd be able to cut off Gug's kidnappers.

The kids held on for dear life as Felix bounced the Zamboni across the snow covered grass. The massive machine smashed through park benches, knocked over picnic tables and drove right over a birdbath.

"Aaaaagh!" Olivia cried.

"Wheeeeee!" Sophie shrieked with joy.

"We're gonna get 'em!" Theo said as they bore down on Artie Sneed's car.

But the Zamboni just missed, clipping the back of Artie's car, causing it to skid, but it soon righted itself and continued on its way.

"There's Gug!" Theo shouted.

Gug, still covered in the net, was looking out the back window at his friends.

"Tutu! Save Gug!" he called to them, clearly scared.

"Step on it, Felix!" Sophie shouted. Felix did.

Artie's beat-up Oldsmobile raced around Town Square, over Crooked Creek Bridge and down Fulton Street. Amazingly, as it flew past Ferro's Delicatessen, the Zamboni was closing in, right behind Artie's back bumper.

Just then, Mr. and Mrs. Bartlett exited Ferro's carrying eight boxes of Christmas pies, cakes, black & white cookies, holiday creampuffs and cannolis. The boxes were stacked so high, that they didn't see the car and the Zamboni go speeding past.

"Here, let me help you with those," said a friendly female voice as the boxes were removed from Mrs. Bartlett's arms. "I'll just put them on the hood of your car while you fish out your keys."

Mrs. Bartlett was about to say "Thank You" when she realized the Good Samaritan was none other than Mrs. Bottleman—the woman that Theo said had abandoned Gug so that she could go on a Christmas vacation to Tahiti.

Mrs. Bartlett instantly saw red.

"Mrs. Bottleman? Back from Tahiti so soon?" she said accusingly.

"Excuse me?" Mrs. Bottleman asked confused.

"Don't play dumb with me!" Mrs. Bartlett pounced.

"Um, dear, take a deep breath—" Mr. Bartlett tried in vain to calm his wife.

"I have no idea what you're talking about," Agnes Bottleman said cautiously, taking a step away from a wild-eyed and red-faced Mrs. Bartlett.

"Like heck you don't! How could you take your family on a winter vacation to Tahiti and leave a poor, lonely exchange student alone for the holidays! And to make matters worse, you come back early and don't even tell him! Gug is a lovely boy—and your loss has been our gain, you ... you ... *mean person!*"

"Okay, darling, let's watch the language," Mr. Bartlett suggested timidly, as he had never seen his wife this angry before.

"Pardon me," Mrs. Bottleman huffed, "But I have never been to Tahiti, I don't know who this Gug person is and I have never, *ever*, had an exchange student in my home. Now, if you'll excuse me, I have cookies and milk that need to be left out for Santa."

Mrs. Bartlett's face changed from red with anger to crimson from embarrassment as Mrs. Bottleman stormed off.

"Well, um ... Merry Christmas, Agnes," she called off feebly, but something told Mrs. Bartlett that she would soon be taken off Mrs. Bottleman's Christmas card list.

"That didn't go so well, did it?" Mr. Bartlett said softly.

Mrs. Bartlett turned to him, her suspicions on high alert. "I think we need to have a talk with our children."

But little did she know that at that exact moment her children were streaking across Mr. Warren's cornfield in a Zamboni, hot on the trail of a 1984 Oldsmobile that was carrying an alien! Felix had become quite good at steering the Zamboni and since it was made to move on ice, the frozen-over cornfield allowed it to move at a great clip. Add in the fact that Artie Sneed hadn't put new tires on his car in nine years and it was obvious why the vehicles were only inches apart.

"Up ahead!" Theo called out, pointing to something in the distance.

"Got it!" Felix shouted.

Felix slammed the accelerator and the Zamboni lurched forward, smashing into the back bumper of the car.

"Hey!" Artie called out in protest.

"What is he? Crazy?" Winston screamed.

But Felix rammed the back bumper again.

"Get him, Felix!" Sophie wailed.

"He's gonna send us right into that … snow bank!!!" Artie shouted.

And that's exactly what Theo and Felix wanted. Artie's Oldsmobile crashed headfirst into a massive snow back, plowing so far into it that both Artie and Winston couldn't open their front doors to get out.

"We're stuck in here!" Winston bawled.

"Climb over the seat! We'll use the back doors!" Artie exclaimed.

But when he and Winston turned to make their move, a large net was thrown over them courtesy of Gug who had spent the entire car ride freeing himself from the trap.

"Aaaagh!" the two kidnappers bellowed as Gug wagged a disapproving finger at them.

"You no nice. You *both* dillweeds."

The back door flew open and Gug turned to find …

"Liv-A!" he yelled! Olivia quickly pulled him from the car as the other children ran over.

"Gug, are you okay?" Sophie asked.

"Gug ok," he answered. "Gug want to go back Soapy's home."

"Ok, let's go," Sophie said, taking the alien's hand.

"Ummm, I think we can do better than just taking you back to <u>our</u> home," Theo said wide-eyed, pointing up to the stars.

They all looked up and saw what Theo was looking at—bright multi-colored lights in the sky, just over the cloud coverage.

"Family!" Gug roared, jumping up and down. "Family! Family! Family!"

"It's the spaceship! It's heading for the woods! They saw our signal!" Olivia exclaimed.

"If I cut all the way across the farmland, we can get there in time!" Felix said.

They quickly clambered back into the Zamboni and raced off, leaving Artie and Winston in a dark, cold car, struggling to free themselves from their very own net.

CHAPTER 31

LADIES AND GENTLEMEN:
THE FLYING ELVIS!

THE SPACESHIP HURTLED through the sky, making it's way toward the signal.

"We're almost there," Donk informed everyone as he held onto the ship's steering column with all his might. The ship was bouncing and shaking like a bowlful of Jell-O on a trampoline.

"Hey!" Elvis pleaded as he gripped tightly to a handrail to keep from falling, "Can't you smooth out the ride a bit?!"

"It's not my fault," Donk explained. "It's natural turbulence that you get from leaving one galaxy's atmosphere to enter another. You're going to have to hold on!"

But the turbulence was much rougher than Donk expected and he was suddenly very glad they had dropped the children off at his sister's hydrogen pod right after they saw the signal. The weather was getting a bit nasty and the ride was too treacherous for little ones.

Just as Donk completed that thought, the spaceship hit an air pocket and plummeted five hundred feet in less than a few seconds.

"Yeeeeooooow!" Elvis wailed as his hands slipped from the handrail, causing him to fly across the flight deck, past Santa (who was bear-hugging a metallic support pole) and into a giant red button that was under a protective glass case.

Unfortunately, the case was not designed to withstand elf-impact, so it shattered and Elvis slammed into the button, pressing it all the way down.

"Noooo!" Matto cried. "That's the Main Power Override!"

"What does it do?" Elvis said as he stood up, broken glass crinkling under his elf-shoes.

But before anyone could answer, there was a loud powering-down sound that filled the ship. It sounded like the last few seconds of noise a vacuum cleaner makes after it is turned off. Then the spacecraft stopped moving ... and then all the lights slowly faded off.

"Oh," Elvis surmised quietly in the dark. "It powers the ship."

CHAPTER 32

WANT A JOB DONE RIGHT?
DO IT YOURSELF!

"WHAT HAPPENED?" THEO worried, looking up at the sky. "The lights went out!"

The children had been waiting at the sleigh in the woods for a few minutes already and the lights had seemed to be getting closer and closer ... and now they were gone!

"Give it a moment," Olivia said. "Maybe they just hit some cloud coverage."

They all stared hopefully up into the sky. Minutes passed. Nothing happened. Then several more minutes. Still no lights. Almost fifteen minutes passed and no one had said anything.

"Family?" Gug finally said softly. A trickle of icy blue liquid streamed down his cheek. It was an alien tear.

"They must've gotten lost and turned the wrong way," she said softly, heartbroken for her friend.

"They were so close," Felix said, dejected.

What none of the kids could have known was that the spaceship wasn't that far away at all and that it took a full twenty minutes to re-boot the ship's power source after the Power Override button had been activated. Motta and Donk just needed a few more minutes to get the ship up and running again and then they could follow the source of the signal light down to the woods, right to where Gug was waiting!

But, back on Earth, the flashlights feeding the signal began to flicker— just a little at first, and then some more, and then ... they went out.

"We lost the signal," Olivia said.

"Well, we have no more gas. Besides, does it even matter? The spaceship missed the signal anyway," Theo pointed out.

"Guess we can only go home now," Olivia said sadly.

The kids all turned to leave. They began trudging through the snow but Sophie soon realized that someone was missing.

"Gug?" she said as she looked back to find the alien picking up presents from the ground and angrily throwing them back into the sleigh. "What are you doing?"

The little guy was sad, but he was even more determined.

"Gug no get family. Kids no get Christmas. Is no right!"

"Gug, there's nothing we can do about it," Theo reasoned.

"*No*. Santa no here. Then *we* do Christmas!" Gug climbed into the sled and began untangling the reigns.

"Yes!" Sophie yelled, climbing into the sleigh to help her pal. "_WE_ do Christmas!"

"Are you out of your mind, Sophie?!" Olivia hollered. "We're just kids! We can't deliver Santa's presents!"

"If we don't, who will?!" Sophie answered, totally fed up. "We couldn't get Gug home. We couldn't get Santa back. Let's at least have one thing go right for us tonight! Let's save Christmas!"

The three older kids all looked at each other, unsure of what to say.

"Heck, I drove a Zamboni—how much harder can a sled be?" Felix shrugged. "I'm in."

He climbed into the sled and got a high five from Sophie and Gug.

"Do you think it's even possible?" Theo asked Olivia. "Because if you say it is, then I'll believe it."

Olivia smiled. It was a wonderful compliment to get, but it was especially wonderful to get it from her big brother.

"Well," she set forth, "There's always a chance. But unfortunately, I don't think there's much of a chance without the reindeer."

"Oh yeah, the reindeer," Theo said, realizing that despite their noble intentions, there was not much they could do without the reindeer to make the sleigh fly.

"Maybe this does something," Sophie said, pointing to a gold button on the front of the sleigh with an engraving of a reindeer on it. She pushed it and the first five notes of "Here Comes Santa Claus" echoed throughout the woods. She pressed it again. And again. And as the notes chimed magically in the air, all around the woods Santa's reindeer woke from their slumber or raised their heads from the creek from which they were drinking or turned from the berry bush where they were eating—and all of their ears perked up. It was *the call*—it was Christmas Eve and it was time for them to do what they were trained for.

The children and Gug marveled as the reindeer slowly entered the clearing from the woods and approached the sleigh. They looked at the children curiously and wondered where Santa was, but they were instinctive animals and could tell right away that these children had good intentions. They did not fuss or struggle at all as their harnesses were placed on them.

The children and Gug buckled themselves in and Felix took the reigns.

"You ready, guys?" he asked the others. "'Cause I can't guarantee how this is going to turn out."

"We can do it," Sophie said looking up at her brother. "We have to try."

Theo nodded.

Felix yanked the reigns tightly and yelled "Heeeaaah!" not because he thought that was the right command for the reindeer but because it was the only thing he'd ever seen done in cowboy movies.

The reindeer slowly moved off, toward the clearing, pulling the sleigh away from the tree into which it had crashed. Once there was some open space, the animals began to pick up speed. Soon they were going incredibly fast. The kids all held on tight as the sleigh began to lift off the ground.

They ascended into the sky at a sharp angle. The night wind whipped strongly into their faces. Felix's hat blew off his head and when he turned back to try to grab it he saw that they were already at least five hundred feet in the air and still climbing. The hat kept falling to the ground and eventually disappeared from view.

CHAPTER 33
YOU NEVER KNOW WHO YOU'LL
RUN INTO IN THE WOODS

"WHAT THE HECK is that?!" Mr. Bartlett asked as they pulled their car into the driveway.

He had noticed—as it was next to impossible to miss—a four-ton Zamboni parked diagonally across his lawn.

"Those kids are in <u>so</u> much trouble," Mrs. Bartlett growled as she jumped from the car and headed toward the house. "I'm going to ground them so long they'll forget what the outside looks like."

"Um, honey," Mr. Bartlett said, his eyes spotting something. "I don't think you should look for them in the house."

Mrs. Bartlett turned toward her husband to find him pointing to several sets of footprints. They started at the Zamboni and led right into the woods. The Bartletts ran along the trail of footprints all the way past Old Face Tree, up and over Miller's Hill and along Crooked Creek. Finally the prints ended underneath some evergreens next to a clearing.

"I don't understand," Mr. Bartlett huffed and puffed as he hadn't run that far in the snow since he was a boy. "The footprints just end. Right here. But where could they have gone?"

"Look at this," Mrs. Bartlett called out, pointing to the sleigh tracks that stretched across the clearing and then just stopped.

They both followed the tracks to where they ceased.

"How could the tracks just end here?" Mr. Bartlett wondered. "They couldn't just float away. Let's go back home. I'm calling the police. Something isn't right here—"

KA-CHUCK! The massive beam of light that hit the clearing was accompanied by a noise that sounded like a huge machine turning on—and that's because it <u>was</u> the sound of a huge machine being turned on. And that machine was a gigantic spaceship. And that spaceship was right above the Bartletts!

Mr. and Mrs. Bartlett were too stunned to speak. They just clutched onto each other, frozen in fear as the craft lowered itself from above and landed gently in the snow of the clearing.

"Are we actually seeing this?" Mrs. Bartlett asked.

"I—I think so," her husband answered.

A door to the craft opened and shadowy figures slowly made their way down a ramp toward them.

"Honey," Mr. Bartlett whispered seriously. "If they want to eat our brains, I'll go first."

"Okay," Mrs. Bartlett answered, just as serious.

Finally, breaking through the shadows and the vapor generated from the ship's reverse thrusters, the first figure emerged. The Bartletts held each other even tighter and braced themselves for …

"Santa Claus?" Mr. Bartlett asked.

"Ho, ho, ho," Santa bellowed.

Mrs. Bartlett took one look at him and fainted.

A few minutes later, when Mr. Bartlett was able to revive her, he explained everything as Santa had explained it to him. He introduced his wife to Elvis and then to Matto and Donk. After getting over the initial shock of meeting Santa Claus, meeting two worried alien parents was almost not that stunning to Mrs. Bartlett.

"So your boy, is he about this tall and talks like this? *More cook-a-goo please*," she said trying to do her best Gug impersonation.

"Yes, that's my baby!" Matto cried. Donk held a translator so everyone could be understood.

"It's ok. He's alright. He's been staying with us," Mrs. Bartlett reassured.

"Oh thank you!" Matto shrieked and she hugged Mrs. Bartlett with all her might. Mrs. Bartlett hugged back. She looked at her confused husband. "It's a mother thing," she explained.

"But where is he now?" Donk asked.

"That's the question," Mr. Bartlett said. "He was with our children and we followed their footprints into the woods and then saw these sleigh tracks here."

Santa knelt at the tracks and studied them. His face grew worried.

"Great Christmas Cobbler!" he exclaimed. "They took the sleigh! They're trying to deliver the presents themselves!"

"*They what?!*" Elvis and Mr. and Mrs. Bartlett all shouted at once.

"This is bad. This is very, very bad!" Santa fretted, pacing in the snow. "They have no idea how fast those reindeer can go. And at night. In severe weather. Your children are in danger and we have to help them! We can track them down from the ship! Let's go!"

But when they all turned to get onto the spacecraft they found their path blocked.

"None of you are going anywhere," Jimmy Flint beamed, a pair of handcuffs hanging from his finger. Chester stood nervously behind his brother.

"James Flint?" Santa queried. "Is that you? I haven't seen you since—"

"—Since you *winked* at me when I was ten! Since you ruined Christmas by promising me a Commander Cody Retro Rocket With Optional Bonus Boosters that never came!"

"Why, James," Santa explained calmly, "I never promised anything."

"You *winked*! A wink's a *promise*! A promise for the most special gift ever and you broke it! I thought I was an important kid for you to single me out like that—but instead I was just another little punk getting a stupid catcher's mitt!"

"Don't one of you guys have a ray blaster or something to take this jerk out?" Elvis asked Matto and Donk who both just shook their heads.

"That won't be necessary, Elvis," Santa said, never taking his eyes off Jimmy. "You were important to me, James. *All* children are important to me. That's why I *did* give you the most special gift I could—"

"A catcher's mitt?" Jimmy scoffed, unimpressed.

"Chester," Santa addressed the younger Flint sibling. "Do you remember what I got you for Christmas that year?"

Chester was so excited—he couldn't believe he was actually about to talk to Santa.

"Yes, Santa. By the way—*Hi Santa*. And yes, Santa. You got me a pitcher's glove."

Santa looked to Jimmy. "The most special gift I tried to give you that year was the gift of your brother, Chester. He worshipped you when you were little, James. But you never seemed to have the time for him. I thought if the two of you played catch together, well, maybe you would have seen what a friend—what a *gift*—you had in your baby brother."

Santa then picked up some snow and blew it in the air. The white powder seemed to hang in front of Jimmy's face for a spell and in it, Jimmy saw moments from his childhood. He saw Chester following him down the street at his side, hanging on Jimmy's every word, looking at his brother with nothing but adoration. He saw Chester running to the sidewalk with hydrogen peroxide, cotton balls and Band Aids when Jimmy had fallen from his skateboard and skinned his knee. He saw Chester saying his prayers at night, asking God to especially look after his big brother.

And then the wind blew the snow dust and the memories away. Jimmy stood there, his face wet with tears. He turned to his brother, sobbing like a baby. "I'm so sorry, Chester! I've been such a bad brother!"

He hugged Chester who cried tears of joy. "That's okay, Jimmy!"

"I love you," Jimmy cried like a baby.

"I love you too!" Chester cried back.

"Ah, the power of Christmas," Santa smiled. "Now, I'm glad you two are all squared away, but we need to get into this spacecraft. A group of children are trying to make my deliveries for me tonight. They are in great danger and they have a big head start!"

"I have a better idea," Jimmy grinned. "If you <u>really</u> wanna catch up to those kids, how 'bout we do it in an fighter jet!"

"You'll do that for us?" Santa asked. "Won't you get in trouble with the Air Force?"

"A spaceship landed on American soil tonight while we were supposed to be on watch. I think I'm <u>already</u> in trouble with the Air Force. Now let's hurry! My truck's just outside of the woods!"

The group trudged as quickly as they could through the snow, across the woods and eventually saw the truck a little bit in the distance.

"There it is," Elvis pointed.

But as they approached the vehicle and were ready to pile in, Winston and Artie Sneed emerged from behind a large boulder, each holding hockey sticks as weapons and garbage can lids as shields.

Santa recognized them both immediately.

"Winston Polenski and Arthur Sneed?" he frowned disapprovingly. "You two were always on the Naughty List."

"Yeah, well, I was never a fan of yours either," Artie cracked disrespectfully.

"You were a disgrace to the red suit," Santa chastised.

"Man, I can't stand you guys who get _so_ into the job," Artie snapped, as he had no idea he wasn't talking to a Shopping Mall Santa but instead was insulting the real Santa. "I couldn't care less about the dumb Santa suit. Or Christmas. Or anything else for that matter except that little green jerk that escaped from me tonight!"

"My baby!" Matto cried.

This caused Artie and Winston to finally notice Gug's parents, who were in the back of the crowd, blocked from view by Santa and Elvis, Jimmy and Chester and Mr. and Mrs. Bartlett.

"Holy guacamole," Winston said in a stunned whisper as he took in the grown-up aliens.

"Looks like it's gonna be a _Green_ Christmas this year," Artie smiled. "If they were gonna give me _one_ million for a little alien, I'll get at least _double_ that for these two big ones here. Now you two, you're comin' with me."

He made a move toward Matto and Donk but Jimmy, Chester and Elvis quickly blocked his path. Winston and Artie held up their shields and hockey sticks menacingly.

"We'll beat you into pulp and leave you all here in the snow!" Artie warned.

Everyone froze. They knew Artie and Winston were bad guys—bad enough to use violence and seriously hurt someone. But they also couldn't let Gug's mom and dad get kidnapped. Mr. Bartlett stepped forward toward the two villains.

"Okay, listen, let's all take it easy here for a minute," he said in a soothing voice. "If you want the aliens, you can have them … but first *how about a little magic trick! ALAKAZAM!!!*"

Mr. Bartlett whipped his arms down toward the ground with all his might. The smoke pellets released from his sleeves at just the right moment and struck the ground at the perfect angle. POOOOF! Smoke exploded all around Artie and Winston causing a huge grey cloud that prevented them from seeing Santa, the aliens and even each other.

"Get in the truck!" Jimmy yelled.

As everyone hurried in, Artie and Winston swung their hockey sticks wildly and blindly.

Mr. Bartlett just kept shouting excitedly "I did it! The Big Goodbye! I finally did it!" as Mrs. Bartlett pushed him into the back seat.

"I knew that Magic Set I brought you in 1981 would pay off one day!" Santa cackled shutting the truck's door behind him.

"I got one of 'em! I got 'em!" Winston shouted as he knocked someone to the ground, sat on their chest and beat them with a hockey stick.

But when the truck raced off and the dust cleared, Winston looked down to find he was on top of Artie Sneed.

Dazed from the beating, Artie lifted his head up and looked at Winston. "Man, I hate Christmas," he said before collapsing back down into the snow.

CHAPTER 34

SANTA CLAUS–ACTION HERO!

"WHOA!" THEO GULPED as he held tightly onto the handrails of Santa's sleigh.

"Sorry—the ride's getting a little bumpy!" Felix screamed over the blaring winds, but Theo could still barely hear him.

The truth was the ride was more than just "a little" bumpy. The weather had gotten incredibly rough and only seemed to worsen by the minute. With each jolt and twist of the sled, it felt as if the children would be thrown out of their seats and into the black night sky. They were buckled in tight and despite the fact that they were all pretty scared up there, hundreds of feet in the air, they were determined to get the job done. They were determined to save Christmas!

Olivia had found Elvis' notebook under the seat. It had charts and graphs and maps with arrows and numbers signifying longitude and latitude and drop locations and a million other details that most kids would never be able to figure out. But most kids are not Olivia Bartlett. She quickly deciphered the elf's plans and explained them to Felix who was trying his hardest to control the sleigh in the blustery winds.

According to the notebook, Santa had planned to begin his route just outside Northern Ontario in Canada so that's where they were heading. But with the bad weather they were hitting, Theo was secretly worried if they'd even make it there alive. They had entered a powerful snowstorm and Felix could barely see where he was going. The reindeer fought through the weather but the sleigh was rocking viciously to the left and to the right, bucking violently up and down! It felt like they were on a roller coaster except the coaster's track was one hundred stories below them! Even Sophie, who normally wasn't scared of anything, gripped Gug's hand tightly.

Just then, a powerful gust lifted the sleigh upward and then slammed it back down, snapping Olivia's seat belt and sending her flying over the side!

"Liv-a!!" Gug shouted at the sight of his friend falling to her certain demise.

"Help!!" Olivia cried. The kids quickly looked over the edge to find that she had managed to grab onto the sleigh's runners at just the last moment. She was holding on for her life—the only thing between her and a thousand foot fall was the strength of her right hand and it didn't seem that strength would last too long.

"Try to keep it going steady!" Theo called to Felix as he got on his belly, his arm reaching down over the side!

"Grab my hand!" Theo yelled.

"I can't! It's too far!"

A heavy gale shoved the sleigh sideways, sending Theo sliding through the small door opening in the side of the sleigh and over the edge to his doom until ... Gug *snatched* Theo's ankles and braced his feet against the inside wall of the sled!

"Gug no let Tutu go!" the alien declared with determination. "Get Liv-a!"

Theo put all his trust in Gug. "Lower me down some more," he ordered Gug.

Gug did as he was told and soon the only parts of Theo's body that were still inside the sleigh were the tips of his sneakers. He swayed back and forth in the storm, which had now grown to a blizzard, and tried to get his hand to meet his sister's. One false move—one whip of wind—and Sophie would become an only child.

Theo knew this and he was terrified. But he wasn't about to let his fear stop him. Not when Olivia needed him.

And the truth is, he would've been even more terrified if he knew that an Air Force jet was barreling down on the sleigh at almost three thousand miles per hour!

"Up ahead, through the snow, I think I see them!" Chester hollered from the co-pilot's seat. Jimmy squinted and spotted them too.

"Good job, bro! Nice spot!"

Chester swelled with pride. He had been waiting for a compliment from Jimmy since he was a little kid—and now that he got one, it was better than he ever could've imagined.

But as the plane got closer to the sleigh, everyone could see something was terribly wrong.

"*Oh my goodness!*" Mrs. Bartlett screamed as she saw her two oldest children dangling in the middle of the air in the midst of a storm.

"We have to do something!" Mr. Bartlett shouted.

"Do you have exterior speakers on this thing?" Elvis asked Jimmy. "We can instruct them down to the ground!"

"A first-timer trying to land a reindeer-powered sleigh in the middle of a blizzard?" Santa scoffed. "They'll kill themselves. No, there's only one way … James, take the plane directly above them."

And as the plane roared faster and upward, back down on the sled Theo was finally able to grab hold of Olivia's hand.

"Ok, I got you!" Theo bellowed, still hanging upside down from the sleigh. "Now you have to let go of the runner with your other hand so I can pull you up!"

"I can't! I'm scared!"

"You can do it!"

"No I can't!" Olivia called back up to him, eyes wide with fright. "You might drop me!"

"I'm scared too! Look at me!" Theo hollered. "I'm hanging by my ankles and the only thing keeping me alive is a four-foot dude from another planet! But I trust him! Now you trust *me*!"

He looked right through all of the darkness and snow and locked eyes with Olivia. "You're my sister, Liv. I love you. I won't let you go!"

She nodded at him, took a breath and then slowly uncurled her fingers from the runner. She instantly was blown toward the back part of the sleigh by the force of the wind! Theo held on with all his might; it felt as if his arm was being pulled from his socket! Gug tried to brace his knees but the weight of holding up two kids at once was taking its toll and gravity was beginning to beat out Gug's will power. He began to slowly slide toward the sleigh's door opening and, as a result, Theo and Olivia dropped further down into the abyss. Sophie wrapped her arms around Gug from behind and pulled as hard as she could but she was too little. They were seconds away from all of them going over the side!

Theo looked down at Olivia. She never took her eyes off her brother. She believed in him. He could see that. There was no way on earth, or a quarter mile above it, that he was going to fail her.

He pulled up with his arm with all of his might, with a strength he didn't know he had, a power that seemed to come from the deepest part of his being. His bicep burned and his shoulder ached but someway, somehow, he began to lift his sister up toward the sled. Eventually, he had raised her enough where he could grab her forearm with his other hand and pull her up onto the sleigh. He collapsed backwards, exhausted. Olivia rolled over onto her back and lay next to her brother a moment, catching her breath.

Theo patted Gug's hand—his way of saying "thank you" when he was too winded to actually talk.

"I love you too, Theo," Olivia said softly.

"Love?" Gug asked Sophie confused.

"It's how you feel *in here* about your family," Sophie said tapping her chest, right above her heart. Gug seemed to instantly grasp the concept.

"Uh, guys," Felix stammered. "I don't think I can control this thing much longer!" The sled was bucking like a wild west bronco and Felix was at a loss at to how to stop it.

If they had a chance to speak at that moment, they all would have agreed that they were done for—that there was no way they were going to figure out how to safely land in such a brutal storm. But, as it turned out, before any of them could say anything, the thunderous engine of a jet plane ROARED overheard.

"Ga-goo!" Gug yelled, pointing upward.

About fifty feet above them was Jimmy's jet—even through the blinding snow storm there was no mistaking it. They all watched in awe as a side hatch slid open on the plane. A figure appeared in the doorway but none of the children could make out whom it was. If visibility had been better that night they would have seen it was Santa and he was about to do something very …

"Crazy!" Elvis argued. "This is crazy—plain and simple!"

"There's no option," Santa said.

"There's no **parachute!**" Elvis stressed. "And even though you're magic, you still need reindeer to fly!"

"There are children down there who need me," Father Christmas said matter of factly. "And has Santa ever let a child down?"

"Not me, Santa!" Jimmy called from the cockpit. "Now I realize you didn't let me down when you gave me the catcher's mitt! Right, Santa?!"

"Oh shut up!" Elvis scolded the Airman.

"Don't worry, Elvis. I'll make it," Santa said as he turned toward the open doorway and looked down at the sleigh twisting and turning far below. He readied himself for the leap, but then turned back to his head elf with a serious look on his face. "But just in case … the spare key to the toy factory is under Dasher's water dish."

Then he winked and jumped out of the plane!

Theo was the first one to figure out what was happening.

"Oh man! Someone's jumped and they're coming this way! Everyone make room!"

The kids scattered to all four corners of the sleigh and covered up, except for Felix who was still trying to steer.

"Aaaaaaaaaagh!"

SPLAT!

Santa landed face down on the sleigh with a thud. The children, who had closed their eyes as they anticipated impact, opened them slowly to find Kris Kringle standing right before them. They were speechless.

"Well hello, children," Santa said. "License and registration, please."

The kids just stood there, mouths open. Even Gug.

"That's just a little joke," Santa smiled.

The wind snapped hard again, shaking the sleigh like a maraca.

"Whoa," Santa said, steadying himself like he was standing on a surfboard. "First things first, let's get this thing on solid ground." He stepped over to Felix. "You mind if I take the reigns for a while, pal—though you are a natural reindeer jockey."

"Yes sir, Santa. I mean, no sir, Santa. I don't mind," Felix said nervously.

Santa took over control of the sled and called out to his reindeer. "Okay, boys, I'm back!"

The reindeer instantly responded to his voice. They snorted and pawed in delight. Blitzen turned back and let out a joyous grunt. Then Santa snapped the reigns triumphantly and expertly guided them back to the woods of Millbrook Falls.

CHAPTER 35
GOODBYE

THE SLEIGH WAS parked carefully in the clearing next to the spaceship, which was parked carefully next to the jet plane. It looked like the world's weirdest parking lot.

The children still could not believe that they were actually in the presence of *Santa Claus*. It was just as crazy as being in the actual presence of *three* aliens.

Gug's parents had gotten so excited when they saw him that they both sprayed gunk all over the place. Then Gug sprayed gunk as well. It shot up into the air, onto the snow, the sleigh, the plane ... and everyone's shoes. No one cared. They were just so happy to see the reunion.

Mr. and Mrs. Bartlett were angry with the children for putting themselves in such danger, but they were so glad the kids were safe and sound that they kept it to themselves. No point in handing out punishment on Christmas Eve—especially when the kids' hearts had always been in the right place.

"Well, this has been quite an evening," Santa said, "but I think these children need to get in their beds. And I need to get to work. Bit behind tonight—luckily I've got fast reindeer and a bit of magic on my side."

He shook all the children's hands. "Thank you all," he smiled. "You have all been put on the Permanent Nice List."

He chuckled as he and Elvis climbed back into his sleigh. They waved goodbye to everyone, but before taking off, Santa reached under his seat and pulled out a box.

"Funny," he said with a sly grin. "This should've been delivered years ago."

He tossed the box to Jimmy who looked at it and then back up at Santa who had already grabbed the reigns and was calling out to his reindeer.

"Dash away all!" he sang and the animals were up and out of sight in a matter of seconds. Nothing was left in the sky but a streak that resembled the tail of a shooting star.

"A Commander Cody Retro Rocket with Optional Bonus Boosters!" Jimmy screamed, as he pulled the last of the wrapping off the gift. "Two of them!"

He gave one to Chester with a smile. Chester glowed.

"I think it's time that we go as well," Donk said to Gug. "Your brothers and sisters are at Aunt Yibglop's and they will be very excited to see you."

Gug turned to the Bartlett children, the realization hitting him that he would never see them again.

Sophie stepped to him, tears in her eyes.

"I'm going to miss you so much," she said, her voice cracking as she cried.

"Me too," said Olivia sadly.

"I wish you could stay," Theo said.

Gug looked at them. He had such strong feelings for them but he wasn't sure how to express it.

So he pointed to his chest like he had seen Sophie do on the sleigh.

"Gug *love* Liv-a," he said looking at Olivia, tapping right above his heart.

"Gug *love* Tutu," he said to his pal Theo, once again tapping his chest.

"And Gug *love* Soapy," he said softest of all, an icy blue tear streaming down his cheek.

He looked at Mr. and Mrs. Bartlett and respectfully said, "Thank you."

The Bartletts nodded back, their hearts breaking. They were going to miss this strange little addition to their home.

Felix waved. "Bye, Gug," he said.

"Bye, Fuffa."

Gug took his parents' hands and headed for the spaceship. They got to the ramp and were about to board when Gug stopped. He turned back and looked at the Bartlett children.

Then he ran to them.

They ran to him as well.

All three kids fell to their knees as Gug collapsed into their arms. They hugged each other tight.

"Gug will miss you. You Gug's family too," he whispered so that only they could hear.

The children said nothing back—they didn't have to—Gug knew how they felt about him.

After a while, the children knew they had to let Gug go. In a week full of difficult moments, this was the hardest one of all.

But they were happy that their friend was back with his parents.

They wiped away their tears and waved good-bye as the spaceship quietly hovered off the ground and cruised out into the stratosphere.

Sophie wanted to stay until the lights of the ship could no longer be seen, so they did. And once the lights were gone, they all headed into the woods.

On the walk home, the children spoke of their adventure.

"I saw Santa, an elf, aliens and drove a sleigh *and* a Zamboni. That's a pretty full night," Felix commented.

"I almost died tonight," Olivia said.

"Me too," Theo agreed.

"I saw seven reindeer butts," Sophie added.

Everyone looked at her.

"I did. They were pointed right at us on the sleigh and their tales go straight up!" she explained. "It was gross."

"Well," Mrs. Bartlett said. "I think that's enough talk of elves and sleighs and reindeer butts for one night. We need to get Felix home and everyone needs a good night's rest. Tomorrow's Christmas after all."

"Thanks to you guys," Mr. Bartlett added proudly.

And later that night, after Felix had been dropped off, and teeth had been brushed and PJ's put on, and foreheads kissed after tuck-ins were complete, the Bartlett children all drifted off to sleep.

And as they slept, they dreamt not of sugarplum fairies, but instead of a unique little friend they had made.

A friend they would never forget.

A friend they would think about often over the years, as they grew older.

Especially at Christmas time.

And who knows? Maybe they hadn't seen the last of him after all.

CPSIA information can be obtained at www.ICGtesting.com
Printed in the USA
BVOW03s1418311214

381525BV00003B/694/P

9 781941 536278